A CUTE

I turned the words over in my head. For some reason, they made me angry—and I knew they shouldn't have. I'd been hearing that same kind of garbage for years. Everybody—perfect strangers, classmates, teachers, even my own little sister—assumed that Miles and I were going out. Miles and I had both learned to live with it, but sometimes it was a royal pain. Why couldn't people just accept the fact that a guy could be my *friend* and nothing else? That's all he was: a friend. Plain and simple.

Don't miss any of the books in *Love Stories*
—the romantic series from Bantam Books!

A Kiss
Between
Friends

Erin Haft

BANTAM BOOKS
NEW YORK · TORONTO · LONDON · SYDNEY · AUCKLAND

To J. S. Wollman

RL 6, age 12 and up

A KISS BETWEEN FRIENDS
A Bantam Book / October 1997

Produced by Daniel Weiss Associates, Inc.
33 West 17th Street
New York, NY 10011.
Cover photography by Michael Segal.

ISBN: 0-553-57078-1

Published simultaneously in the United States and Canada

Bantam Books are published by Bantam Books, a division of Bantam
Doubleday Dell Publishing Group, Inc. Its trademark, consisting of the
words "Bantam Books" and the portrayal of a rooster, is Registered in
U.S. Patent and Trademark Office and in other countries. Marca
Registrada. Bantam Books, 1540 Broadway, New York, New York 10036.

PRINTED IN THE UNITED STATES OF AMERICA

OPM   0 9 8 7 6 5 4 3 2 1

ONE

SAM

THERE IS A certain time of year—a certain moment, really—that everybody knows and dreads. It's the moment you first start to notice how the breeze is getting a little colder, the sunlight is starting to slant a little more, the leaves are starting to droop . . . and *boom!* Suddenly the fun is over. Bye-bye summer. Hello panic, homework, cram sessions, exhaustion—all the good stuff that comes with the fall. And as I walked down Guadalupe Street with Miles that Sunday afternoon, I realized for the first time just how unexpectedly fast that moment can arrive.

"I can't believe it's already fall," Miles groaned. "I can't believe we're actually going to be seniors. Tomorrow."

I had to smile. Miles Wilson and I always seem to be thinking the same thing at the exact same time. Or *saying* the same thing at the same time. Or not saying anything at all. Sometimes it almost feels as if we're psychic or something. There's a definite intuitive, unspoken

1

language between us—almost like an invisible connection between our brains. Then again, if you've been hanging out with the same person every single day since the seventh grade, that kind of thing is probably normal.

"Hey, it's not so bad," I said dryly. "Just think. As seniors, we have the added bonus of college application freak-out."

Miles just shook his head. "Ugh. Don't remind me. Please let me enjoy my last day of freedom in peace."

"Freedom?" I asked, raising my eyebrows. "Miles, give me a break. As of tomorrow, *I'm* the one who is going to be slaving through basketball practice every afternoon. But as soon as that final bell rings, you're free to do whatever you want."

Miles just smirked. As I said, we have an unspoken language—and a lot of it depends on sarcasm. He knew that I didn't regard practice as any kind of cramp on my freedom. One of my greatest pleasures in life— aside from teasing him—is playing basketball. In fact, I had babbled all summer long about how thrilled I was to finally get the starting point guard position.

"You're right," he said wryly. "I *am* free to do whatever I want. I've gotta stop hanging out with those fools in the art studio and get a real hobby."

I rolled my eyes. Although few people know it, Miles is an amazing sculptor. For some reason, he insists on keeping his work private. If *I* were that talented, I'd go around bragging about it to every single person within shouting distance.

He works with clay. Over the years, my room has grown cluttered with dozens of his pieces: little

2

elves, dragons, and an oversized hand palming a tiny basketball (my personal favorite). I'm always trying to get him to set up an exhibition, and he's always giving me the same answer: He isn't ready. I've never believed him. Ever since he was a freshman, he's spent every single afternoon in the art studio at our school, hanging out with these two other artists and working on new projects. And each new piece he shows me is better than the last one.

"Seriously, though," I said. "Where *are* you thinking of applying?"

"UCLA, remember?" he said. "We both are, Sam. They have a great basketball program. See, I have it all planned out. By the time we graduate, you'll be the first woman ever to be drafted into the NBA. Then I'll be your agent." He cupped his hands over his mouth and spoke in a quick monotone, imitating a sports announcer. "Scott takes the inbounds pass with two seconds left . . . she shoots a three-pointer for the tie . . . she misses! What a choke! Crazed fans beat her to a pulp—"

I slapped his arm, pretending to be offended, though I couldn't help but laugh along with him. Miles Wilson's laugh is highly contagious. His lips start to twitch, his bright brown eyes start to twinkle, his hair starts to shake—and then when he really gets going, his wispy brown bangs inevitably end up in his face. It's . . . well, cute. In a very goofy sort of way.

"What about you?" he asked after a moment. "Where are *you* going to apply?"

I shrugged. "Wherever you are," I said—and I

meant it. I hadn't really allowed myself to think too deeply about college. That was because I didn't want to consider the possibility of being apart from Miles.

Miles and I had first met at the video arcade on West Twenty-fourth Street. We were both twelve years old. We played each other in Wrestlemania—and of course I whipped him, thereby earning his undying respect. From that moment forward, we were inseparable. Back then we even *looked* alike: tall and skinny with short hair and baseball caps. Eventually, however, I lost the baseball cap and let my red hair grow past my shoulders. And yes, though it's hard to believe, I even developed a taste for those flowery summer dresses that are sold only in thrift stores, dresses like the one I happened to be wearing that very afternoon. But the tomboy reputation never quite went away. When your best friend is a guy and you spend a lot of time trying to put a ball through a hoop, these kinds of silly labels have a way of sticking.

"Well, one thing's for sure," Miles said. "I'm psyched to get out of Austin." He glanced around at the crowd of young people milling past us on Guadalupe Street. It seemed as if everyone under the age of thirty had decided to spend the last day of summer the way we were spending it—namely, wandering around aimlessly.

"You really want to leave? But Miles." My voice grew deadly serious. "Austin is the next Seattle."

Miles cast a sidelong glance at me. Then we both started cracking up.

"Austin is the next Seattle" is a big inside joke

among nonmusicians at Jefferson High. That's because every single kid who plays an instrument has said those words at one time or another. It's like some kind of secret catchphrase or something. The hip crowd is convinced that the next big musical trend is going to start in Austin, the same way grunge started in Seattle and went on to sweep the nation. As far as I can tell, nothing big or trendsetting is really happening here among kids our age—but still, over half of the student body now own a guitar.

Miles sighed. "You're right," he said in a dull voice. "I don't think I could live with myself if I missed the rise of the next Pearl Jam."

"Yeah. Maybe we should stay." I slipped my hand around his arm to avoid being separated from him as we snaked our way through the mob. "It would be kind of fun to be the next Seattle. Maybe we'd even get our own Space Needle. Or at least a basketball team."

Miles grinned. "Speaking of which, the Supersonics *are* looking pretty good this year."

I frowned. "I thought you were a Bulls fan."

"You see, that's another good thing about Austin," he replied evenly. "You can root for whatever team you want. You're not tied to any home court. And this year I'm going to be a Supersonics fan. Or maybe I'll go for the Houston Rockets." He nodded to himself. "Yeah, I could see myself really getting into the Rockets."

"Mmm-hmmm," I said. That was a very typical Miles thing to say. He's always floating from one obsession to the next. That summer, for instance, he had been obsessed with motorcycles. He'd had this huge plan about how we were going to drive around the country after graduation on a beat-up old "hog" (that's really what he called it, much to my dismay) with a little sidecar attached. Then he'd promptly forgotten all about it. I could see the same thing happening with the Rockets. I was just about to make the comparison when Miles froze in his tracks.

"Sam, you're not gonna believe this," he whispered. "Look!"

I followed the direction of his outstretched finger. He was pointing at a big window directly to our right. The window belonged to Phineas Bloom's Vintage Clothing. And there, behind the glass, were two of the most ridiculous motorcycle helmets I had ever seen. They were covered with sparkles and featured matching American flag motifs: stars, stripes, the whole works.

"We have to buy those," Miles announced earnestly.

I blinked. "We do? Why? Are we planning to go on *Soul Train*?"

"No!" he cried. "Don't you get it? *That's* what we're going to wear when we live out our big dream."

For once in my life, I had no idea what Miles was talking about. "Uh . . . you wanna clue me in again on what our big dream is?"

He shook his head and looked at me as if I had lost my mind. "What do you think, Sam? Our big dream is to roam the country next summer on a hog with a little sidecar attached."

"Ohhh." I bit my lip to keep from laughing. "*That* big dream. I thought you had forgotten about that.

You know, I was actually just about to remind you—"

"Come on," he interrupted, tugging me toward the door. "We're going to buy those right now."

I kept my arm looped under his and my feet planted firmly on the ground. "Miles, I can't buy those," I stated. "I mean . . . um, I'm broke." I actually had about twenty dollars on me—but there was no way I was going to let *him* know that.

"That's okay," he said. "You can just pay me back."

I started laughing. "Miles, you don't get it. I'm *not* gonna wear one of those helmets. I'd rather risk death than wear one of those."

"Come on!" he exclaimed, unable to keep from laughing too. "Just picture it. We're cruising down the highway out of Vegas." He pulled his arm out from under mine and held out his hands, revving an imaginary engine. "You're in the sidecar. I'm—"

"And why would *I* be in the sidecar?" I asked, trying hard to sound indignant.

"Because," he said matter-of-factly, "you don't know how to drive a hog." He went on, clearly lost in his own fantasy world. "Anyway, Mafia hit men are chasing us. We've just made forty grand at the craps table. I kick the hog up to ninety-five—"

"I'll tell you what," I interrupted. "I'll think about buying one of those helmets if you promise me you'll stop saying the word *hog*."

He let his hands drop. "You'll *think* about it?"

"Miles, we'd probably be arrested if we were caught wearing those." I gestured toward the window. "Just *look* at them."

He nodded very calmly. "I'm looking. And I'm seeing two of the coolest, baddest, meanest-looking helmets I've ever laid eyes on."

I moaned. "I hate to break it to you, pal, but this is 1997, remember? Those were obviously made during the most heinous days of the seventies. They went out of fashion about the same time *The Brady Bunch* went off the air."

"Sam, helmets like those *never* go out of fashion," Miles declared. "So are we going to buy them or what? I promise I'll stop saying hog."

"Well . . ." I took one last look at the window. A little grin curled on my lips. It actually *would* be pretty funny to cruise around in those helmets. He nodded excitedly, reading my expression. I shook my head. For some inexplicable reason, Miles can usually get me to go along with almost every outrageous idea that pops into his brain.

"So?" he prodded.

"Okay, okay," I relented. I glanced furtively around the crowded street. "But can we come back some other time and get them? I don't exactly want to lug them around right now."

"I don't know," he said dubiously. "Somebody might come along and want them as bad as we do. . . ."

"I doubt it," I muttered. I took his arm again and tried to pull him away from the window.

"Can't we just go in and see how much they cost?" he protested.

At that moment the door opened. A balding hippie type with a long gray beard poked his head

8

outside. "I couldn't help but notice y'all were checkin' out the his-and-hers motorcycle helmets," he said in a raspy voice. "I'll sell 'em to ya right now for fifteen bucks apiece."

Uh-oh, I thought. Before Miles could open his mouth, I quickly said, "Thanks, but we don't have the money right now."

"That's okay." The man flashed a yellow grin. "If you really want 'em, I'll let you put a ten-dollar deposit down. That'll reserve them for three months."

I wanted to offer an excuse, but Miles was already fishing a crumpled ten-dollar bill out of his pocket. "Thanks a lot, man," he said, slapping the bill into the guy's hand. "I appreciate it." He winked at me. "We both do. We'll be back to pick them up soon."

"Great." The man chuckled. "Here's a receipt." He pulled a scrap of paper out of his shirt pocket and scrawled his initials on it. "A cute couple like you two shouldn't go without a set of dynamite gear like that. I'll see y'all real soon." He handed the paper to Miles and disappeared back into the shop.

Miles and I looked at each other blankly for about a split second. Then he cracked a smile. I started giggling. Before I knew it, we were both laughing hysterically.

Finally I took a deep breath. "Let's get out of here," I mumbled, praying that the guy hadn't seen us. I took his arm once more and we headed back down the street.

"Wow," Miles said. "I'm telling you, fate must have wanted us to have those helmets." His voice took on the dramatic edge it always does when he thinks he's on the verge of some huge revelation. "It's a sign that we must live out our big dream."

"Miles, it wasn't fate who wanted us to have those helmets," I said. "It was a fat old hippie guy looking to make some cash."

"How can you say that?" he cried, but he was smiling. "You don't have any faith, Sam. That's your problem. But I'll tell you what. We'll make a deal. Let's buy each other the motorcycle helmets sometime during the next three months. That'll take care of our Christmas presents for this year. And it—"

"Christmas presents? Nice try. There's no way I'm going to let you weasel out of getting me a Christmas present by putting five more bucks down on a star-spangled helmet."

He sighed. "Sam, Sam, Sam," he said, shaking his head as if he were talking to someone half his age. "It's not the money or the present—or even the helmet itself. It's the symbolic nature of the act. When we exchange those helmets Christmas Day, we'll be making sure that the road trip will happen."

"Right," I said. "There's only one problem. We still don't have a motorcycle with a sidecar."

"All in good time," Miles replied. "The helmets are the first step. We'll save up money for the next nine months and buy the rest of the stuff after graduation. Right now we just have to make sure that you get the 'his' to give to me and I get the 'hers' to give to you. . . ."

I let Miles ramble on for a while longer about the helmets, fate, the big dream, et cetera, but my mind was drifting. I couldn't help thinking about what that guy had said just before he'd gone back inside his shop: "*A cute couple like you shouldn't be without a set of dynamite gear like that.*"

A cute couple. I turned the words over in my head. For some reason, they made me angry—and I knew they shouldn't have. I'd been hearing that same kind of garbage for years. Everybody—perfect strangers, classmates, teachers, even my own little sister—assumed that Miles and I were going out. Miles and I had both learned to live with it, but sometimes it was a royal pain. Why couldn't people just accept the fact that a guy could be my *friend* and nothing else? That's all he was: a friend. Plain and simple. My best friend, true, but . . .

"What are you thinking?" Miles suddenly asked.

"Oh, I was just thinking about how that guy is probably gonna sell those helmets anyway," I lied.

Miles shook his head. "No way," he said. "It's fate, Sam, remember?"

I laughed softly. "Right."

He stopped then and looked me straight in the eye. "We *are* going to live out our big dream, aren't we?"

I paused for a moment, returning his gaze. With his wide brown eyes glistening in the late afternoon sun and that hopeful smile on his face, he reminded me of an eager little kid who desperately wants to be told that there really *is* a tooth fairy or that Santa really *does* exist. I had a wild urge to promise him anything he wanted to hear just to preserve that adorable expression.

But instead I just shrugged. "I hope so, Miles," I said, without any commitment. "I sure hope so."

TWO

MILES

THE FIRST DAY of my senior year was possibly the dullest day of my life. Maybe it was because I had been expecting to feel some kind of excitement—or at least a sense of superiority, knowing I was older and wiser than three-quarters of the school. But there was nothing. Zilch. Once again I simply wandered through the same old tired routine like a robot: getting my textbooks, listening to my first homework assignments, and answering lame questions about my summer.

Of course, it didn't help that Sam and I weren't in a single class together. We had always shared *something*—usually a class that never should have been invented in the first place, such as chemistry. But since we had each fulfilled most of our requirements, we were more or less free to take what we wanted . . . and it was pretty obvious by the end of the day that we wanted to take totally different things. But I guess it wasn't all that surprising. Sam usually got bored in art classes, and I was taking two of them, as well as art history.

It was only after the final bell rang and I walked out of eighth-period Spanish that I began to feel better.

"Mr. Wilson?" a deep and unmistakable voice called.

A smile broke out on my face. I turned to see Mr. Washington, my former art instructor, making his way toward me down the hall.

"So you managed to survive another summer," he said. "Congratulations."

Mr. Washington was by far the coolest teacher at Jefferson. He must have been in his early fifties (he refused to reveal his age), but he acted a lot younger, or at least a lot less stuffy, than the rest of the teachers. I always thought that he bore an un-canny resemblance to James Earl Jones, that guy who does those commercials for the Yellow Pages. The only big difference was that Mr. Washington had thick grayish white hair and a goatee. He was the one who had first encouraged me to use the art studio after school to work on my sculpture.

"How's it going?" I asked.

"Can't complain," he said with a smile. "You know, I was hoping I'd catch you before the end of the day. I already ran into your hoodlum friends. They promised me they'll be making a mess of the studio again this year. What about you?"

By my "hoodlum friends," Mr. Washington meant Ryan Lee and Kirk Evans. Ryan and Kirk were the other two kids who spent their afternoons in the art studio during the school year. Both were painters, but they had very different styles. Ryan concentrated on landscapes. Kirk was a portrait painter who painted mostly in black and white. Like me, neither one had exhibited his work to more than a few people. And like me, neither one could decide on which NBA team to root for.

"As a matter of fact, I'm headed there right now," I said. "I can't let those chumps take up all the good space."

Mr. Washington chuckled. "Nothing ever changes with you guys. I'm going to the studio myself. Come on."

As we climbed the stairs to the third floor, I actually began to feel pretty good. Over the summer I had almost forgotten how much I loved working in that cramped little paint-splattered room along with Ryan, Kirk, and Mr. Washington. I've never understood the theory that artists prefer to work in perfect solitude. It's no *fun* if you're all by yourself. Then again, maybe that's why I've always been such a mediocre artist.

"You got any projects in mind this year?" Mr. Washington asked.

I shook my head as we strolled down a deserted hall to the far end of the building. "Not really."

"Did you sculpt at all this summer?"

"A little," I said, feeling slightly embarrassed at my lack of productivity. "I guess I wasn't really inspired. I spent most of my free time hanging out with my best friend."

He nodded. "Well, sometimes it takes a familiar environment to get back into the swing of things."

He paused outside the studio door and smiled. "But you won't be coming back here forever, you know."

"I know," I said, and for the first time all day, I felt like a real live senior. It was scary.

Ryan and Kirk were already in the tiny studio, setting up their easels—and taking up most of the floor, of course. They had shoved the clay table back against a wall, sandwiching it between the kiln and the big closet where all the smocks were kept. There was hardly any space left for me to work. I couldn't help but snicker.

"What's up, boys?" I asked. I tossed my book bag on top of the clay table. "Thanks for leaving me so much room. It's good to see you guys haven't changed."

Actually, they *had* changed—or at least Ryan had. It looked as if he hadn't cut his thick black hair since the spring, and now it was pulled behind his head in a long ponytail. His face was scruffier too. I smiled. Maybe he was trying to look more bohemian or something. Kirk, however, still looked pretty much the same, which was the exact *opposite* of bohemian. He was big and bulky, and his short blond crew cut was even shorter. He looked more like a prizefighter than an artist.

"Hey, man, first come, first served," Kirk said. A sardonic grin crossed his face. "You should know that by now, Miles. You gotta move fast."

Ryan patted my shoulder. "So, Miles, how was the summer?" He flashed a quick glance at Kirk. "You still seeing that girl Samantha?"

I had to laugh—and they started laughing too.

"Man," I said. "It's amazing. You guys are still

using the same old lame material. You'd think that after three months, you could come up with something more original."

Kirk shook his head. "What about *you?*" he asked. "Are you still going to play it like you and Sam Scott are just 'friends'?" He emphasized the last word and made little quotation marks in the air. For a brief instant, even though I hadn't seen him in three months, I felt a strong urge to punch him in the face.

"Seriously," Ryan said, reaching into the closet for a smock, "that stuff has gotta end."

I slouched against the clay table and folded my arms across my chest. "And why's that?" I asked.

"Because we know you're going out," Kirk said.

I raised my eyebrows. "Oh, yeah? How do you know that?"

Ryan and Kirk exchanged glances again.

"Miles, we saw the two of you yesterday down on Guadalupe," Ryan said. He looked at me as if I were guilty of a crime. "You were obviously hanging out . . . you know, *that way*. And I know about these things."

I nodded slowly. "I'm sure you do, Ryan. But you guys were hanging out together too, right? Maybe somebody is thinking the same thing about *you* two right now."

"That's funny, kid," Kirk said dryly. "You can still make 'em laugh. But I doubt anybody's thinking that. Ryan and I weren't walking arm in arm."

"Not to mention the fact that we were with Kim and Sara," Ryan added. "Unlike you, we aren't afraid to admit that we *are* going out with our girlfriends."

"You know, Miles is right," Mr. Washington grumbled. He was standing over by the art studio's battered little boom box, rummaging through a crate of old cassette tapes. "You guys haven't changed one bit. You still gossip like my grand-daughter's friends—and she's in kindergarten."

But Kirk and Ryan just kept right on smiling. "Come on, Miles," Ryan said. "Give it up. It's time to come clean."

I shook my head. At first I had been amused, but now I was starting to get depressed. I definitely needed to find a girlfriend—if only to get Ryan and Kirk to shut up about Sam once and for all. Maybe working alone *wouldn't* be such a bad thing.

"Believe me," I muttered, "the second I start going out with someone, you guys will be the first to know." I pulled a smock from the closet and listlessly tied it on, then crouched down by the little refrigerator where the clay was kept. *At least I have clay,* I thought glumly, opening the door and examining the semester's fresh supply. *Clay never comes up with wild theories about my nonexistent love life.*

Kirk sighed. "Well, pal, if that's the way you want to keep playing it, that's okay. Although personally, I don't know *why* you're ashamed to admit that you're going out with Sam Scott. If you ask me, I think she's pretty hot." His voice grew dreamy. "I mean, she's al-most like a model . . . all tall and thin, with those big blue eyes and that long red—"

"I know what she looks like, Kirk," I growled. Hearing Kirk Evans salivate over my best friend was *not* going to elevate my mood. I grabbed a piece of wire off the table and cut a hefty sliver of clay from the big square lump inside the fridge, then slammed the door shut.

"Not to mention the fact she can probably whip any of us on the basketball court in a game of one-on-one," Ryan added quietly.

"You guys?" I said. I stood up and gave them each a big fake smile. "You can feel free to shut up at any time." I turned around and began hurling the clay repeatedly at the table in order to get the air bubbles out of it. The violent, repetitive motion, accompanied by the loud *thwack . . . thwack . . . thwack*, was very satisfying—and, I hoped, at least slightly threatening.

"Seriously, though, Miles," Kirk said in a very unserious voice, "I just want to say that it's good to see you. You know, even if you don't want to admit what's going on with you and Sam. It's great to be back, isn't it?"

"Oh, yeah," I muttered. "Great."

Before either of them could make any more wise comments, Mr. Washington put a tape into the boom box and pressed the play button. Horribly cheesy seventies music instantly filled the room. I laughed once. I couldn't decide which was worse—being tormented by Ryan and Kirk, or listening to *this*. Over the summer, I'd also conveniently forgotten about Mr. Washington's dismal taste in music.

I glanced over my shoulder at Ryan and Kirk. They both made gagging motions.

"Hey, um, Mr. Washington?" Kirk asked. "Do

you think we could listen to something *besides* disco this year?"

Mr. Washington sighed disappointedly. "This isn't *disco,* Mr. Evans. It's Curtis Mayfield. And since this is *my* studio, we're going to listen to *my* music. When you guys have *your* studios, you can listen to *your* music."

Ryan looked at me, then back at Mr. Washington. "Curtis who?"

"Never mind." Mr. Washington turned the music down a notch. "One of these days I'm going to have to teach the three of you to appreciate the finer things in life."

"It better wait until after graduation," I said. "We should probably just leave the music off until then. I don't think my brain has enough room to appreciate any more new stuff right now. Especially the finer things."

Mr. Washington snorted. "If you didn't put so much effort into being a clown, Miles, maybe you'd find some room left in that brain of yours." He turned the music down a little more, then looked at the formless hunk of clay sitting on the table. "As a matter of fact, why don't you use what brainpower you can spare to try something new and different for your first project? Try something you've never done before."

I glanced at the clay. Even though I didn't want to admit it to him, I was still feeling completely uninspired. I didn't want to disappoint him either. One of the coolest things about Mr. Washington is that he always treats these little after-school sessions as informal workshops—advising us, making suggestions, offering critiques, and pushing us to improve. But my mind was blank. I had no idea what to sculpt.

"How about trying to sculpt a bust of someone you know?" Mr. Washington suggested, sensing my hesitation. "A three-D version of what Mr. Evans here specializes in."

An image of Sam immediately popped into my mind. It would actually be pretty cool to try to sculpt her head—or maybe even a miniature of her whole body. I'd never tried it before. I could even sculpt her wearing one of those red-white-and-blue motorcycle helmets. Then maybe she'd feel obligated to wear one in real life.

"Yeah, that's a good idea," Kirk agreed. He and Ryan were already busily applying the base coats of paint to their canvases. They clearly had projects in mind—which made me feel even more pressured to think of something fast.

"You know, you could do a sculpture of Sam," Kirk added. "I've done tons of portraits of Sara. Girlfriends are always good subjects." He paused and gave me a deadpan look. "Oops, I forgot. She's not your girlfriend."

I just scowled at him. On second thought, sculpting Sam—at least *there*—would probably be a big mistake. I turned back to the ugly, damp little grayish lump. There had to be something I could make. . . .

My thoughts were suddenly interrupted by a high-pitched screeching noise from the hall. It sounded like microphone feedback.

The four of us shot bewildered looks at each other.

Then there was a low buzzing noise, followed by the loud, muffled thumping of drums. A second later, guitars joined in. All at once, the walls of the art studio were shaking with the music of some very bad punk rock band. Ryan, Kirk, and I started laughing.

"What *is* that?" Ryan yelled over the din.

Mr. Washington's brow wrinkled. "The music department moved some of its practice rooms up here over the summer." He frowned at the door. "I guess they're letting student bands rehearse here after school."

Kirk shrugged. "At least it drowns out Curtis Mayflower."

"May*field*," Mr. Washington growled.

"I'll go ask them to turn it down," I offered, stepping quickly toward the door. I was actually glad to have an excuse to leave the room. It would give me some more time to procrastinate.

"Careful," Ryan warned. "You might go deaf."

Outside, the music was even louder. It wasn't hard to find the room where the band was playing—the noise was coming from behind a large metal door at the opposite end of the hall, near the stairs. I knocked a few times. I don't know what I was thinking; they obviously couldn't hear me. Finally I just pushed the door open.

The music immediately stopped. Three vaguely familiar kids in flannel shirts and torn jeans were staring at me from behind their instruments.

"Uh, sorry to barge in on you like this," I mumbled. "But do you think you can turn it down? It's just that we're working in the art studio. . . ."

"Uh, sure," the drummer said unenthusiastically. The other two looked slightly embarrassed. "Sorry. We're getting soundproofing tomorrow. We'll keep it low."

"Thanks a lot."

I closed the door behind me. That had been easy enough. But as I walked back down the hall I heard another sound. There was a conversation coming from another one of the rooms—a classroom two doors down from the art studio. And even though I don't usually like to eavesdrop on people, I couldn't help but listen. Besides, they *were* talking loud enough for me to hear them, now that the music had stopped.

". . . can't talk about this anymore right now," a guy was saying. "I have to go in there and start practicing. They're waiting for me."

"Connor, they can *keep* waiting, all right?" a girl snapped. "Don't you think this is important?"

Connor, I thought. I knew right then that the guy must be Connor Smith, the self-appointed king of Jefferson's alternative rock scene. He was a pretentious schmuck. He was probably the one who had coined the phrase "Austin is the next Seattle."

"I'm sorry, baby, but that's all I have to say," he said. "I just need some time off. I'm a senior, okay? The band thing is starting to happen. I need my freedom."

I almost felt like laughing. *Baby?* He couldn't be serious. He sounded as if he were playing the part of the sleazebag in some really bad after-school special. "*The band thing is starting to happen. I need my freedom*"—how clichéd could you get?

22

"That is such crap," the girl hissed. "You're a selfish jerk, you know that? I mean, if this is the way you want to end it after all the time we spent . . . Look, just forget it. You can *have* your freedom, whatever *that* means."

I slowed to a snail's pace as I approached the classroom door, which was ajar. As much as I hated to admit it, this was actually pretty interesting.

"China, don't get all wigged out on me—"

Connor's voice was cut short by the sound of a chair scraping against the floor. Angry footsteps pounded toward the door—and the next thing I knew, I found myself face-to-face with the most beautiful girl I had ever seen.

She paused and stared at me.

I held my breath. Her name was China Henry; I knew that much. She was short and slender and delicate. I had never paid much attention to her before because she had always hung out with the musician crowd. But for the split second that she stood in front of me, I took in her every feature. Her grayish eyes were flecked with little streaks of brown. Her lips were very full and red, and her soft skin was flushed, as if she had just been running. Long curly chestnut hair cascaded over her cheekbones and hung well past her shoulders. She had tied some of it into a single braid on one side. There was a thin silver hoop in her left nostril.

She was amazing.

Our eyes locked.

Her lips seemed to quiver.

And then she went storming down the hall.

23

Almost instinctively, I whirled around to watch her.

"What the hell are *you* looking at?" a harsh voice barked in my ear.

I glanced over my shoulder to see Connor Smith glaring at me. Over the summer he had bleached his short, spiky hair platinum blond. He looked like a fool. I didn't even bother answering him. I turned back to catch a last glimpse of China—but she had already disappeared down the stairs.

"Mind your own damn business," Connor muttered. He marched past me to the practice room and slammed the door behind him.

For a moment I just stood there in the empty hall, frozen in place. Then I let out a deep breath.

"Whew," I whispered. I shook my head. What on earth did a girl like China see in a guy like *him?* I wandered back into the studio, my mind in a fog.

"Did you tell those guys that we're trying to appreciate the finer things in here?" Kirk asked.

I barely heard him. "Uh . . . yeah," I answered absently. I immediately went for the clay and began kneading it, working it intently with my fingers, making it easier to shape.

Mr. Washington chuckled. "You look like a man on a mission, Miles. You suddenly get inspired or something?"

The image of China Henry's face flashed into my mind's eye, as clearly as if I were looking at her photograph.

"Like never before," I murmured.

THREE

SAM

BY THE TIME I got home from basketball practice, I was seriously ready for another summer vacation. Every joint in my body was throbbing with pain. I hadn't even known I *had* so many joints. My bones were creaking. I lumbered slowly up the stairs to my room, feeling like an eighty-year-old woman.

"Sam, is that you, honey?" my mom called cheerily from the kitchen.

All I could manage was a long, low moan.

"How was your first day back?" she asked.

"Tiring," I croaked. "I'll tell you about it later." I stumbled into my room and immediately collapsed into bed.

For a while I just lay there, listening to my lungs heave. Why did Coach Manigault have to start right away with a *three*-hour practice? Couldn't she have eased us in slowly? And I wasn't the only one teetering on the verge of death at that moment. Ariel Conrad, my best friend on the team, had driven me home in the same miserable condition. It was pretty clear she hadn't bothered to keep in shape over the summer either.

"Dinner will be ready in about fifteen minutes," my mom yelled from the bottom of the stairs. "Okay, dear?"

"Okay," I called back uncertainly. At this point, even the *thought* of dinner was enough to make me queasy.

I rolled over on my side and glanced at the little nightstand next to the bed. My old, worn leather-bound diary was sitting there next to the telephone under the soft light of the lamp. Not once had I ever failed to enter a little passage about the first day of school—and I'd had the diary for almost six years. A vague feeling of guilt passed through me. I figured I had to write *something*. It was a ritual. But I barely had the energy to keep my eyes open, let alone lift a pencil and put it to paper.

After staring at the book a little longer, I finally managed to summon enough strength to reach for it. I sat up against the pillows. If I couldn't write, at least I could read. I opened to a section from a few years back and turned the pages until I found what I was looking for.

Monday, 7:25 P.M.
Well, freshman year started with a bang.
I got sent to the principal's office. It wasn't
my fault, of course. Miles was making some
weird face at me during algebra. I laughed
so hard that I fell out of my chair. Principal

Craft was really cool about it, though. She said that people sometimes have a hard time adjusting. I just smiled and nodded.

I must say, high school is totally different from what I expected. I guess I thought that everyone was going to be a lot more mature or something. But people are just as lame and giggly as they were in the eighth grade. And, of course, I'm the worst. No, on second thought, Miles is the worst. He never gets caught for anything. Luckily I only have three classes with him. If I had any more, I would probably flunk out of Jefferson.

A smile spread across my face—partially out of amusement and partially out of embarrassment. Looking through my old diary entries always made me feel funny. I never seemed to be able to do it without asking myself if I was really *that* much of a loser. I flipped ahead to the same day the next year.

Monday, 8:37 P.M.

Summer is over. I can't believe it. I know sophomore year is going to be a disaster. I walked into first-period chemistry only to discover that Miles was there too. After five minutes (count 'em, five) we got yelled at. Miles was whispering something about the teacher's toupee and, well, the rest is fairly obvious. We aren't allowed to sit next to each other for the rest of the

year. I think it's part of his one-man con-
spiracy to get me expelled.

On a happier note, I think I may start on
JV this year. If I get the spot, Ariel and I will
be the only sophomore starters. Hooray!

I groaned. Yes, I *was* that much of a loser. How
could I have been so excited about starting for the
junior varsity basketball team? At that moment, I
wished I had never even heard of the game of basketball. As far as I was concerned, *basketball* was to
torture what *boat* is to *ship.*

I snapped the diary shut and put it down beside
me. My entry for *this* first day of school was going
to be much, much different. First of all, I wouldn't
be complaining about Miles, because I didn't have
any classes with him. Second, I was prepared to quit
basketball forever and join the glee club.

Having no classes with Miles was really kind of a
bummer. The only time I had seen him all day was
at lunch. No wonder I was feeling so lousy. I hadn't
even gotten into trouble once. I grinned tiredly.
School without Miles was so . . . dull.

The phone rang. I was too exhausted to do any
more than just look at it. Luckily, somebody picked
it up in the middle of the second ring.

"Sam!" my little sister's whiny, annoying voice
shrieked from somewhere downstairs. "It's your
boyfriend!"

I rolled over and snatched the receiver off the
hook. "Beth, if you call Miles my boyfriend one

28

more time, I'm personally going to make sure that you don't live to see dinner," I said. "Okay?"

Beth just giggled.

"You can hang up now," I added, a little more curtly.

There was a fumbling noise, then a click. "Miles?" I asked.

"No—it's your boyfriend." He sounded especially cheerful, but maybe that was just because I was feeling so foul. "You know, Beth is starting to remind me more and more of Kirk and Ryan," he said.

"She is?" I frowned. "In what way?"

"Well, for one, she hates disco. And she still refuses to believe that we aren't going out."

I decided not to pursue the disco comment. I wasn't exactly in the mood for Miles's more bizarre brand of humor. "So what's up?" I grunted.

"Jeez. It's nice to talk to you too, Sam," he said sarcastically. "I just wanted to see how the rest of your day was. How was practice?"

"Don't ask." I flopped back against the pillows and closed my eyes. "I am *so* out of shape right now. And Coach Manigault . . . I think she must have watched one too many motivational tapes this summer. She didn't let us take a break once. I just got home like five minutes ago."

"No breaks?" Miles said in a mocking tone. "Come on, Scott. Sounds to me like you've lost that competitive edge. That's not good for a starter."

"Yeah, well, basketball, schmasketball," I grumbled. "So how was *your* day?"

29

"Oh . . . not bad. Same old, same old. I'm trying to think if anything happened . . . Oh, yeah." He paused. "I fell in love."

My eyes opened. I waited for the punch line. None came. "Uh—you want to run that last part by me again?" I asked after a moment.

"I fell in love," he repeated.

"Oh, right," I replied nonchalantly. "You know, I was wondering when you were finally going to admit the truth about you and Kirk Evans."

Miles laughed. "No, Sam, I'm serious. It was like I was struck by a bolt of lightning. I bumped into this girl outside the art studio, and my whole life changed."

"Why? Did she steal your wallet or something?"

"I *mean* it," he said.

"Sure you do, Miles," I muttered. "So who is this girl anyway?"

"China Henry. Do you know her?"

My brow wrinkled. "That little waif who hangs out with the Eddie Vedder crowd? Yeah. I have American lit with her this year."

"She's not a little waif, Sam," Miles stated in a flat tone. "She's beautiful."

I chewed my lip for a second, frowning. Beautiful? There was no way he could possibly be serious. China Henry was attractive, sure—but she was about as far from being his type as someone could get. "You *are* joking, aren't you?" I asked.

"No," he answered simply. "Why is it so hard to believe?"

"Well . . . maybe because you never mentioned her once before in your life."

"I never *noticed* her before. Until this afternoon."

I sat up in bed, forgetting my exhaustion. "Miles, were you sniffing rubber cement today in the art studio? We *are* talking about the same China Henry, right?"

He laughed again. "I know it sounds crazy, Sam. And I really can't explain it. All I know is, when I saw her today, it was like seeing her for the first time." His voice took on an odd, mushy quality. "It was like . . . seeing perfection."

My eyes narrowed. I didn't know whether I wanted to giggle or barf. "Um, do you realize how incredibly pathetic that sounds?"

He didn't say anything.

"Miles?" I asked.

"Hey, I'm sorry I brought it up," he snapped. "Just forget it."

"Oh, brother," I groaned. "Please don't go all sensitive on me right now. I'm too tired."

"All *sensitive?*" he demanded.

"Okay, look, Miles, I'm sorry," I apologized dully. "I'm happy for you. Really. It's nice that you fell in love. Congratulations."

"Yeah, well, now I just need to find a way to talk to her," he mumbled. He sounded more as if he was talking to himself than to me. All at once he perked up. "Hey—you just said you were in her American lit class."

I sneered. "So?"

31

"Well, maybe you could—"

"Pass her a note?" I interrupted. "Forget it, buddy. You're on your own with this one. This isn't junior high. You want to get to know her, talk to her yourself."

"Fine," he said irritably. "I will. It's nice to know you're behind me on this."

I sat there, staring into space, at a complete loss for words. I'd never heard Miles get so testy over something so ridiculous. So he had a crush on some girl. Big deal. And not just any girl, but one who looked as though she came straight out of a Soundgarden video. He needed me to be behind him on *that?* If he couldn't see how lame that was, that was his problem, not mine.

"Look, I better go," he announced abruptly. "I'll see you tomorrow. Have a good night."

Before I could even say good-bye, there was a loud clunk.

"Miles?"

But no one was there. He had hung up.

"Jeez," I breathed. I placed the phone on the receiver and sank back into bed.

I lay there for a few minutes, feeling unsettled and fidgety. Had I just been beamed into some weird alternate universe? That had been one of the strangest conversations I'd ever had with Miles—*ever.* The last time we'd even come close to getting into a fight was at the beginning of the summer. And I couldn't even remember the argument exactly, because it had been so insignificant.

I glanced at the phone. Maybe I should just call him back. But then again, *he* was the one who was acting like a dork. And besides, I was too tired to bother. Knowing Miles, he would just forget about this stupid infatuation in a few days—the same way he would forget about being a Rockets fan and, I hoped, about buying those dumb helmets.

"Dinner!" my mom called from downstairs.

"Coming," I answered automatically. But I was slow to get out of bed. The odd, restless feeling hadn't gone away. Had I been overly harsh with him? I had to admit, I was pretty cranky. And I didn't have any right to judge him. If he wanted to pursue China Henry, for whatever unfathomable reason, that was his business. I'd never meddled in his love life before—not that either of us had been overly lucky in the romance department. No, the state of affairs was pretty sad. Our respective love lives had always been pretty much nonexistent.

In fact, I had never even come close to having a boyfriend, now that I thought about it. A few guys—all of them older and on the boys' basketball team—had asked me out a couple of times in the past, but none of the dates had ever led to anything. Sitting there, I suddenly realized that I'd never even *kissed* a guy before, except during games of spin the bottle in the eighth grade. Not that I'd wanted to kiss any of those basketball players. I laughed out loud. They were all tall, gangly fools. But still, it was a little disheartening.

Of course, Miles hadn't fared much better either.

He'd had one girlfriend. In the tenth grade he'd gone out with some ditz named Jennifer Moreland. It had lasted about a week. She later transferred—but not before she fooled around with almost every healthy male student enrolled at Jefferson. I shook my head. Poor Miles. I'd tormented him relentlessly about it. And even though I had been polite to her, I'd said plenty behind her back. I *had* meddled.

"Sam!" Beth shouted. "We're waiting for you!"

"I'm coming!" I yelled back. I pushed myself off the bed and headed for the door. I would apologize the next day. China Henry, even if she was a social-climbing groupie, was certainly a step above Jennifer Moreland. Miles deserved to go out with somebody this year; we *both* did. I shouldn't have been so obnoxious.

"What's taking her so long?" I heard my mom ask as I walked down the stairs.

"She's probably still on the phone with her boyfriend," Beth whispered loudly.

I grimaced. Maybe I *would* talk to China Henry after all. If I helped set her up with Miles, then maybe everyone would finally shut up. Then again, I couldn't quite picture the two of us striking up a conversation. But at least I would let Miles know that he had my blessing to chase after her, for better or for worse. That would fix the situation.

I sat down to dinner expecting to feel better inside.

But for some reason, I didn't.

FOUR

MILES

I WAS ALREADY sprinting up the stairs to the third floor by the time the eighth-period bell finished ringing—and it was useless. Once again, both Kirk and Ryan had beaten me to the studio. In fact, they were already in their smocks and busily painting. I stood in the doorway, gasping for breath.

"Forget it, man," Kirk said. "You're never gonna get here first."

I shook my head. "I don't get it. Don't you guys take classes? I mean, you are still students here, right? You haven't been kicked out?"

"I have shop eighth period," Ryan said. He dipped a thin brush into the paint on his palette and shrugged. "It only meets once a week."

"Shop? You gotta be kidding me. I didn't even know they still had that." I glanced at Kirk. "What about you?"

"I have eighth period free, Miles," he said,

grinning. "I planned ahead." He jerked his head toward the refrigerator without taking his eyes from his canvas. "By the way, I took a look at your sculpture. It's good. But I think your girlfriend is gonna get jealous."

"I doubt it," I mumbled.

I maneuvered my way through them and dropped my book bag on the clay table, then opened the refrigerator. My forehead immediately wrinkled in disgust. The sculpture of China that I'd started the day before was *not* good, despite what Kirk had said. Looking at it now, with fresh eyes, I could easily see the mistakes: The forehead was too wide, the nose was too small, and the eyes were too far apart. No, it wasn't any good at all. I was going to have to start over.

"So who is that anyway?" Kirk asked.

"It isn't Sam Scott," I replied.

"I *know* that. But who—" Kirk broke off when I began throwing the still-soft sculpture against the table a couple of times, turning it once again into a formless mass of clay. "Hey, what are you doing?" he cried.

"It stinks," I said with a shrug. I rolled the clay into a ball about the size of a large grapefruit. "I gotta start over."

"Man," Kirk said. He looked baffled. "You're way too hard on yourself, you know that, Miles?"

I knelt beside the table and began shaping the clay again. "I'll take that as a compliment."

"Well, don't get *too* cocky." He paused.

"So anyway, you didn't answer the question."

"What question is that?" I asked. I turned my back to him and Ryan so I could get a better angle—and so I wouldn't have to look either of them in the eye.

"If it wasn't Sam, who was it?"

"Somebody I made up," I lied. It's always much easier to lie if you aren't face-to-face with someone.

"No way," Ryan said dismissively. "Nobody works the way you were working yesterday on something they just *made up*."

I dug my thumbs into the clay, working on the eyes first. "And what way is that?" I asked, grunting slightly with effort.

"Like the way you are now," Kirk said. "Like you're totally possessed."

They both laughed.

I stopped and looked at them over my shoulder. "Fine," I stated very calmly. "I'm trying to sculpt the face of somebody I'm in love with."

Ryan and Kirk both frowned. Then they glanced at each other. I quickly turned back around so they couldn't see me smile. It figured: Lying had failed, but telling the truth had worked perfectly. They didn't believe a word of it.

"So . . . what does Sam have to say about all this?" Kirk asked. "I mean, if Sara knew I was painting another girl's face, I'd probably be in big trouble."

"Yeah, well, I don't think she'll really care," I said. It was funny—I hadn't seen Sam once that day, not even at lunch, and deep down I was sort of re-lieved. I'd spent my lunch period at the registrar's office trying unsuccessfully to switch into another Spanish class so that I too could have eighth period free. It had been a waste of time. But if I had eaten with Sam, I knew she would have just told me how idiotic I was being about China Henry. And, of course, she would have been right. I was in love with some girl who hadn't even talked to me yet.

"Hey, Kirk?" I suddenly asked. "How did you meet Sara?"

"Well, we both go to the same high school, Miles." He sounded as if he were talking to a three-year-old.

"No, seriously," I said. I leaned back to study the little indentations I'd made for the eyes. Then I began to work on the cheekbones. "I mean, how did you first get to know her?"

"Well, I always knew who she was, just from seeing her around," Kirk replied after a minute. "I mean, we'd say hi in the halls and stuff. Then last year we were in the same geometry class. We ended up being in the same study group. One day it was sines and cosines, and the next—well, you get the picture."

"That is . . . so . . . *beautiful*, man," Ryan sobbed sarcastically.

I smirked. "What about you?"

"Me?" Ryan asked. "Well, now *here's* a story for you. You see, Kim lives two blocks away from me. I used to see her around all the time, but I never talked to her. Then one day I'm walking home from school, and I notice her sitting on the curb bawling—totally out of control. So I ask her what's wrong. It turns out her boyfriend just dumped her. Anyway, I end up spending the whole afternoon with her, you know, consoling her. Two months later, we were going out."

I turned around and raised my eyebrows. "Are you *serious?*"

"Yeah." He looked at me out of the corner of his eye. "Why?"

"It's just . . . I don't know." But I was thinking about the coincidence: China had just been dumped by *her* boyfriend. Maybe I should have tried to talk to her the day before. But no, that would have been stupid. Connor had been right there. Still, something about Ryan's story made me feel as if I had just blown some kind of opportunity.

Ryan laughed. "Is it really that hard to believe? How did *you* meet Sam?"

"We used to hang out at the same video arcade a long time ago—the one on West Twenty-fourth Street," I said impatiently. "But how long did you wait to ask Kim out after you met her? I mean, wasn't it kind of weird under the circumstances?"

He shrugged. "I guess so. But it didn't take her that long to get over her old boyfriend. He was a serious moron. I guess I must have waited about a month and a half—you know, until she stopped mentioning him completely."

"A month and a half?" I groaned. That seemed

like an eternity. Would it take China that long to get over Connor? After all, he was a moron too. Maybe it would take even longer. Maybe they'd just get back together. . . .

All at once I realized Ryan and Kirk were staring at me.

"What?" I demanded. I quickly turned back to the clay table.

Kirk chuckled. "Why all the sudden interest in how we met our girlfriends, Miles?"

I lifted my shoulders. "I'm curious," I said, knowing that I sounded extremely defensive.

"Look, I may be going out on a limb here, but does this newfound curiosity have anything to with the fictitious girl you're sculpting?" Kirk asked.

My cheeks grew hot. "What makes you think that?"

Both of them were laughing now. "Come on, Miles," Ryan said. "You know you can't hide anything from us. Who is she? Don't worry, we won't tell Sam."

"You won't tell *Sam?*" I repeated incredulously. I'd never heard anything so lamebrained in my life. They thought I was sneaking around behind Sam's back. I was seriously on the verge of losing it and confessing the whole ridiculous truth—or jumping up and pounding them both—when, thankfully, Mr. Washington strolled in.

"Hello, gentlemen." He paused for a second, looking perplexed. "Hey, what's with all the guilty faces in here? You guys in trouble?"

"No, but somebody's gonna be," Kirk said smugly.

Mr. Washington frowned. "You know, I won't even bother asking. I don't want to be involved in your delinquency, Mr. Evans." He glanced at me. "Hey, Miles, would you mind doing me a favor and grabbing a couple of buckets from the supply closet on the second floor? I'd ask one of these clowns, but they already have their smocks on."

"Yeah, sure," I said, hopping up eagerly. I needed an excuse to get out of that little room and clear my head. "No problem."

I shut the door behind me. One of these days I was going to kill those guys. Preferably sooner rather than later. I took a few deep breaths, then began walking down the deserted hall.

Maybe, I thought, I should just start lying and say that yes, I *was* going out with Sam. That would probably make my life a lot easier. Except that if I told those guys that I was going out with Sam, it might somehow get back to China. . . .

I couldn't believe what I was thinking. I was driving myself crazy over a girl who didn't even know I existed—a girl with whom I had shared only a split-second glance. But it had been a friendly glance, hadn't it? In the instant our eyes had met, I'd sensed the beginnings of a melancholy smile. Then again, I do have a pretty vivid imagination.

When I reached the second-floor landing, I suddenly realized something. I didn't even know where the supply closet was.

I stood there for a few seconds, looking idiotically in both directions, when someone came out of a classroom and turned in my direction.

My heart lurched.

It was China.

She smiled as she approached. "Lost?" she asked.

Time seemed to freeze. I blinked a few times, unable to speak or even breathe. She was just as beautiful and perfect as I'd remembered her. She was wearing frayed bell-bottom jeans and a green-and-white-striped T-shirt. Her grayish eyes sparkled. She drew closer. Finally I managed to get a grip on myself.

"Uh, yeah—I am, actually," I said with a nervous laugh. I could hear my heart pounding in my chest. "I'm looking for the supply closet."

She shrugged. "Oh. Sorry. Can't help you there." Then she peered up at me closely. "Hey—your name is Miles, right?"

I nodded, too shocked to respond.

"And you're a sculptor?"

My eyes narrowed. Hardly anybody knew I was a sculptor. The situation was very quickly becoming surreal. I felt as if I were dreaming—or hallucinating. "Well, I wouldn't exactly say *that*," I said. "I mean, I mess around in the art studio after school. How did you know . . . ?"

"Well, your hands *are* covered with clay," she said with a smile.

I looked down at my hands. Sure enough, my fingertips were stained with a muddy gray color. I hadn't even noticed. I started to blush.

"But I know you are anyway," she went on in a practical, businesslike tone. "See, I was talking to Mr. Washington earlier today. I work on the school paper, and this year I was thinking about writing a feature about the school art scene. So I talked to a bunch of art teachers—" Suddenly she broke off and laughed embarrassedly. "Hey, I'm sorry. I don't think we've ever really met. I'm China Henry."

I nodded. "I know. I mean, I've seen you around," I added quickly.

Our eyes met for a moment, then her gaze shifted. She kept talking in a slow, measured voice. Hearing her speak was like listening to music. "So anyway, I thought I would do a story about Jefferson's student artists. And when I talked to Mr. Washington, he mentioned that you and some other guys use the art studio after school to work on your own stuff. I thought that sounded really cool. I've actually been wanting to talk to one of you about it. . . ."

I just kept staring at her.

Finally our eyes locked again. She smiled shyly, twisting her braid with a finger. "So it's kind of lucky I ran into you. Do you think maybe, sometime, we could talk—I mean, if you have some spare time?"

I blinked. My mind seemed incapable of absorbing all she had said. Various thoughts swirled around in my head, in no particular order. China Henry wanted to talk to me. She thought it was lucky I'd run into her. She thought the art studio was cool. All of a sudden I laughed. Maybe if she saw what the art studio was *really* like—with Ryan and Kirk hogging all the space and the three of us talking nonstop trash—she might change her mind.

A look of mild disappointment crossed her face. "Of course, I can understand if you don't want—"

"No, no," I interrupted. "It's just that, uh, I never really, um—you know, I never thought that anybody would be interested in what we do up there."

"Really?" she asked, sounding genuinely surprised. "I can't believe somebody hasn't written about it already."

I forced a smile. My heart was thumping again. *Don't talk like an idiot,* I commanded myself. But I just mumbled, "Uh, gee—well, I . . . uh, I guess it's nice somebody wants to. You know, write about us."

Her face brightened. Her cheeks still had that same flushed glow that I had noticed the day before. "So would you be willing to talk about it sometime?"

"I guess," I said with a shrug.

"Great. I'll be in touch." She gave me one last smile, then started down the hall.

I followed her with my eyes, my jaw hanging open slackly. China Henry—*the* China Henry—was going to be in touch. Things like that didn't happen to me. Usually I had to content myself with torment, misery, and failure. I turned around and bounded back up the stairs. This was a truly momentous occasion.

Sappy disco was playing on the boom box when I burst back into the studio, but for once I didn't mind. "Boys, I've got great news," I announced with a broad smile. "We're going to be famous. Somebody's going to write about us in the school paper."

Nobody said anything. The three of them looked at each other blankly.

Finally Mr. Washington broke the silence. "Uh . . . whatever you say, Miles," he said. "But in the meantime, do you think you could get me those buckets?"

FIVE

SAM

WHAT CAN HE possibly see in her? I wondered for about the hundredth time that morning.

China Henry was sitting two rows up from me and to the left, staring intently at Principal Craft. She was wearing ridiculous vinyl pants and a tiny white T-shirt. She had probably planned the outfit piece by piece months in advance. Her belly button was showing, as usual. She must have gotten all her fashion tips from MTV or something. Miles didn't even *watch* MTV. Well, not very much anyway.

". . . which is why he is enamored of his sister's innocence," Principal Craft was saying.

I tore my eyes from China and forced myself to look toward the front of the classroom. I needed to start concentrating. The whole reason I had even signed up for American lit was because it was the only class Principal Craft taught. I had always liked

Principal Craft, ever since I had been sent to her office that first day of freshman year. She seemed to get along best with the troublemakers. Besides, the books we were going to read that semester looked like the kind of books I might actually enjoy.

"Compared to his experiences in New York . . . ," she went on.

But it was hopeless. I was unable to listen. I didn't even know what she was talking about. Anyway, I couldn't stop thinking about Miles and China Henry.

A whole day had come and gone since Miles and I had gotten into that fight—or whatever it had been—on Monday night. I still hadn't talked to him. I hadn't even *seen* him. I probably hadn't gone thirty-six hours without seeing or talking to Miles in over a year. It was a little disturbing. I had to find him that day at lunch and clear the air.

Suddenly a forest of hands shot up. I glanced around nervously. Then I raised my hand too. I didn't want to look like an idiot.

Principal Craft's eyes roved the classroom. They settled on me.

Uh–oh.

"Ms. Scott," she announced. She peered at me over the rims of her glasses. "You've been rather quiet this morning. Your thoughts on the matter?"

"Uh . . . my thoughts?" I asked tentatively.

"Yes." She raised her eyebrows. "We were discussing Holden Caulfield's relationship with his sister," she prompted.

I swallowed. "Holden Caulfield?"

She sighed. "You *did* read *The Catcher in the Rye*, didn't you? It was on the summer reading list. Your hand was raised."

My mind raced frantically. I was pretty sure I had read *The Catcher in the Rye*—but all I could remember about it now was the plain maroon cover. "Yeah . . . I read it," I said slowly. "It's maroon, right?"

There was dead silence.

All at once Principal Craft burst out laughing, along with several of the other students, including China Henry.

My face turned bright red. So much for trying *not* to look like an idiot. I couldn't believe what I had just said. Not only was I the biggest idiot in that classroom, but I might have been the biggest idiot at Jefferson High—and maybe in all of Austin.

"Well, Samantha, that's the most original description of *Catcher in the Rye* I've heard in a while," she said. "I think you might just have a career writing book reviews. You could organize them by color."

Luckily, the bell rang before she could say anything more. I don't think I had ever been more relieved to hear that sweet, shrill sound in my life. I slumped into my chair, exhaling deeply.

"Tonight I'd like everyone to read the first fifty pages of *Slaughterhouse Five*," Principal Craft announced as people scurried for the classroom door. She held up the book, looked at it, then glanced at me. "It's quite a novel, as you can tell by the cover. Sort of whitish gray, don't you think?"

I put my face in my hands for a second, then stood

up. Principal Craft was shaking her head. I sauntered past her, trying to look as abject as possible.

"Let's try to stay a little more alert tomorrow, Samantha," she said, gently but firmly. "Okay?"

"You got it." I kept my head down as I hurried into the hall—and nearly slammed right into someone a lot shorter than me.

I looked up. It was China Henry.

"Sorry," I mumbled. Unfortunately, any path of escape was blocked by the sudden swarm of kids.

"No problem." She laughed. "You know, I think that was probably the funniest thing I've ever heard anybody say to Principal Craft."

I frowned. Did she think that was some sort of compliment? "Yeah, well, I like to try my new comedy numbers on her," I said flatly.

Her friendly expression faded. "I didn't mean it in a bad way," she muttered.

Oh, brother. Now I felt bad. Even if she was a fool, she had only been trying to say something nice. "Look, I'm sorry," I said. "It's just that, uh, I thought it was kind of embarrassing."

"Embarrassing? No way." She looked directly at me. "Actually, I think I'm going to use that line in another class and take credit for it."

I almost laughed. Maybe she wasn't such a fool after all. "But you can't," I said, smiling. "I have witnesses."

"I'll get my own witnesses," she shot right back. "It won't be the first time I've taken credit for something you said."

I cocked an eyebrow. "It *won't?*"

49

"Nope." She was smiling now too. "Last year I was standing behind you in line this one time at the cafeteria. You took a plate of food and looked at me and said: 'Jefferson pot roast—the *other* gray meat. We're not just for prisons anymore.' I repeated the whole thing to my friends, word for word. They thought I was a genius."

I couldn't believe it. I didn't even *remember* saying that. "Wow," I marveled. "Maybe I should start charging you for my material."

She shook her head. "It's too late for that. Although maybe you really *should* have a comedy act."

"Hmmm," I said. "Maybe you're right."

An awkward silence fell between us. Suddenly I became aware that the hall was a lot less crowded than it had been a minute earlier.

"Well, I should probably get going," we said at the same time. We immediately looked at each other and laughed nervously.

I shifted my gaze to the floor. "Um—actually, I don't have to go anywhere. I have second period free."

"Really?" she said. "Me too."

There was another lull. We glanced at each other again. I thought about Miles. If he'd known I was standing there with the woman of his dreams, he probably would have freaked out. He also probably wouldn't forgive me if I didn't try to keep the dialogue going. Talking to her *would* be an easy way to patch things up between him and me. And she certainly seemed a lot cooler than I had originally thought.

The second-period bell rang.

"So where are you headed?" I asked.

"I was going to the library to do some homework," she said hesitantly. She opened her mouth as if she were about to say something else, then began absently twisting her long, lone braid with one finger. "Um—actually, do you mind if I ask you something?"

I shrugged.

"Your boyfriend is a sculptor, right?"

I started laughing. "You mean *Miles?*"

"Yeah," she said, looking confused. "He's not a sculptor?"

"No, no—he is," I said. "He's just not my boyfriend."

China's face turned pink. "I'm sorry," she mumbled. She tried to smile, fumbling with her braid uncomfortably. "I just thought . . ."

"Hey, it's no big deal," I said. "Everybody thinks he's my boyfriend. What about him?"

She paused for a second. "Uh—you guys didn't just break up or something, did you? I don't want to bother you if, um, it's a bad time. . . ." She let the sentence hang.

"No," I said slowly. "He never *was* my boyfriend." A strange idea crept into my brain. Could it be that *she* was actually interested in Miles? No . . . that was too bizarre to be possible. "People just think we go out because we hang out together all the time. We're friends, that's all. Best friends, I guess."

She shook her head, looking much more relaxed. "Wow. I always assumed . . . you know . . . but I guess everyone else does too."

"I'm surprised anyone even notices us," I muttered, almost to myself.

She chuckled. "Of course they do. You know how people are in this school. They have to make up stories about everyone to keep themselves amused." She shrugged. "I know I do."

I laughed, taken off guard. That had been a pretty honest confession to make to a complete stranger—especially one who had nothing to do with her social scene. I respected her for it. I had always figured that China Henry and her hip friends wouldn't stoop to ponder the life of a lowly jock like me. But, of course, that had just been my way of making up stuff about *them*. China was absolutely right. Everybody acted the same way. Amazingly enough, I had something in common with this girl.

"So what do you want to know about Miles?" I asked.

She took a deep breath. "Well, here's the deal," she said. "I want to do this article for the school paper about artists at Jefferson. Yesterday I spoke to a few teachers in the art department, and one of them mentioned that Miles and two other kids use the art studio after school to work on their own stuff. I thought that sounded really cool. So I wanted to talk to Miles about it."

I shrugged nonchalantly, but I was thinking: *Miles is going to have a heart attack when I tell him this.* "I'm sure Miles would love to talk to you," I said. "I mean, I know he'd be totally psyched just to see his name in print."

"Really?" she asked. She sounded doubtful. "See, when I mentioned it to him yesterday, he didn't seem too thrilled. In fact, he sort of looked at me like I was a crazy person."

"You mentioned it to him *yesterday?*" My eyes narrowed in disbelief. That couldn't be right. There was no way Miles could have met China Henry and *not* called to tell me about it. He always kept me updated on his obsessions, and China certainly qualified as one of the big ones . . . unless he hadn't called me on purpose. Could he have been avoiding me? Had I offended him that much on Monday night?

"Yeah, I ran into him on the second floor, after school had already let out," she said. "He was polite and everything, but I sort of got the feeling that he thought I was wasting his time. He hardly said a word."

I nodded distractedly. I could just picture the scene. Miles had probably been standing there with his tongue hanging out, unable to speak because his hormones were in overdrive, and China had mistaken the silence for lack of interest. It was absurd. "He's just shy," I said after a minute. "I'm sure he'd be willing to talk to you."

"You really think so?"

"I *know* so," I said. My response was a little too emphatic, but she didn't seem to notice. "I'll tell you what. I'll talk to him about it if you want."

"You would?" she asked hopefully. "That would be so cool. I mean, don't make a big deal about it or anything. I can always talk to those other two guys first. I mean, I was planning on talking to all of them at some point."

I shook my head. "It's no problem."

"Great," she said. "Thanks a lot."

I shrugged. Once again there was a pause.

China looked at her watch. "I really should try to do some of the homework I blew off last night," she murmured apologetically.

"Me too," I lied. I was suddenly thankful she had supplied a convenient way for us to end the conversation. My brain seemed to be stewing in a dozen vaguely troubling emotions, none of which I could quite figure out. I needed to be alone to sort through them. "I'll, uh, see you later, I guess."

"Yeah." She glanced up at me with an easygoing smile. "It was nice to actually meet you after all these years. I mean, seeing as I rip off all your jokes."

I managed a grin. "Yeah, likewise. I needed the ego boost."

"I *am* gonna use that line, you know." She turned to go. "Thanks again," she called over her shoulder.

I watched her until she disappeared around a corner. My brow was furrowed, but I was smiling at the same time. Was I actually friends with China Henry now? It didn't quite seem possible. The whole thing with Miles had started because I had refused to talk to China on his behalf—and now I was going to talk to *him* on *her* behalf. I could never imagine something so crazy in a million years. Maybe Miles had been right about that fate stuff after all. Maybe he and China Henry were destined to be together.

Of course, at this point, China wasn't interested in him for anything more than a story in the school paper. I was starting to feel oddly relieved, even though I wasn't sure why. It wasn't as if I didn't approve of her. I liked her a lot, in fact. She *was* Miles's type: smart, funny, even enthusiastic about art. And if I had a belly button like hers, I'd probably show it off all the time too.

I frowned. Could it be that I was envious?

No. I knew I wasn't. Sure, she was pretty, but she was a shrimp. She'd last about two seconds on a basketball court. Besides, my belly button wasn't *that* bad. And there was no denying that most of her friends were lame.

Well, one thing was certain: I needed to talk to Miles. Immediately. No wonder I was feeling so strange and uneasy. This stupid fight had gone on long enough. If he really *was* mad enough to blow me off, then I had to let him know about my little encounter with his ideal girlfriend. After that, he would forget about any kind of dumb argument. I smiled to myself again. In fact, he would probably be prepared to do anything I wanted. Maybe he'd even agree to let the motorcycle helmet issue slide.

Yes. As soon as I told him about China, everything would be back to normal.

SIX
MILES

"SAM!" I YELLED, spying her across the crowded, sunlit cafeteria. She was sitting alone at our old, familiar spot—a small round table with only three chairs, tucked away in a far corner. I weaved in and out of people, struggling to keep a soda and a mystery-meat sandwich balanced on my tray. I felt as if I hadn't seen or talked to Sam in months. Of course, it had been less than two days. But now that I didn't have any classes with her, it was almost as if we didn't even go to the same school anymore.

"Sam!" I called again.

She didn't respond at first. She just looked up and stared at me as if I had totally lost my mind. Then she smiled, looking very puzzled. I placed my tray down on the table and slumped into one of the two free chairs.

"What's up?" I asked breathlessly.

"Nothing." There was an uncertain tone in her voice.

"Is something wrong?" I asked, biting into the sandwich.

"Uh . . . you aren't mad at me?"

"Mad at you?" My mouth was full. The question sounded more like *Ma ah oo?* I forced the food down. "Why would I be mad at you?"

She pursed her lips. "You *did* hang up on me the other night, Miles. And I haven't spoken to you since."

"Oh." I laughed sheepishly. I guess I *had* been a little annoyed, especially after the comment about passing China a note. But that seemed like eons ago. "Sorry about that. I'm not mad. And anyway, the problem's been solved." I took another bite.

"I know," she said, with just a hint of annoyance. "Thanks for calling to tell me about it."

I chewed the rubbery food, squinting at her confusedly. "Tell you . . . about what?" I asked after a minute.

She raised her eyebrows. "That a certain girl wants to write an article about you for the school paper."

My mouth fell open.

"Eew—Miles!" she cried disgustedly. She turned away and held her hands in front of her face. "Will you *please* finish eating? You are so gross. . . ."

A few kids at a neighboring table snickered, but I was too shocked to really notice or care. I swallowed, then gasped, "How did you find out?"

Sam lowered her hands and smiled slyly, as if she had a secret. "Well, I made a new friend this morning—a very nice, waifish girl in my American lit class. You know, the one with the pierced nose? She said she bumped into you in the hall after school yesterday."

I dropped my sandwich back onto the plate, suddenly forgetting my appetite. "You *met* China? What did she say? I mean—what did you talk about?" The words tumbled out of my mouth in a high-pitched rush. I couldn't believe Sam had actually spoken to her. "How did it happen?"

"One question at a time, please," Sam muttered. "Well, for one, she said that I've been her secret comic inspiration for years." She sat up straight, striking a haughty pose. "She said that she steals all my brilliant witticisms and uses them on her own friends, taking full credit, of course—"

"All right, Sam," I interrupted. "What did she *really* say?"

She frowned. "That's what she really said, Miles," she stated. "You can ask her if you don't believe me."

I sighed. "Okay, okay—besides that. What did she say about me?"

Sam rolled her eyes and leaned back in her chair. "Not a whole lot." She sounded bored. "The usual."

"The *usual?*" I demanded. Now I was more than a little irritated. "What's that supposed to mean?"

"The usual, meaning what everybody else at Jefferson says about you," she replied. "That you're my boyfriend."

Irritation turned to horror. "You've gotta be kidding," I breathed. "Why would she . . . ?" I couldn't even finish the question.

Sam's expression soured again. "It's not *that* big a shocker, Miles," she snapped. "Everybody thinks we're going out."

"I know, I know," I muttered. "But it's just . . ." I looked up at her. "You told her the truth, right?"

"No, I told her we were engaged, Miles," she said dully. "Of course I told her the truth."

I nodded, exasperated. "Okay. So what did she say after that?"

"Well, she said that you didn't seem very interested in being interviewed for an article in the school newspaper. She said you looked at her like she was crazy. She honestly thought she was wasting your time."

"I—I—," I stuttered, but then my head drooped. This was just great. Any feelings of euphoria I'd experienced before now flowed out of me completely, like air out of a deflating balloon. So the verdict was in: I had indeed made a complete imbecile of myself the day before. Sam had been right on the phone the other night: I *was* pathetic.

"Hey, don't look so depressed," Sam said encouragingly. "I told her I'd talk to you and convince you to do the article."

I glanced up at her. "You *what?*"

Sam nodded, grinning. "I told her you were shy but that you would love to see your name in print. She seemed psyched."

"She did?" My mood lifted again. "Psyched in what way? I mean, what did she do?"

Sam sneered. "Get a grip, Miles. She wasn't drooling or anything. She just wants to talk to you. She wants to talk to Ryan and Kirk too."

"Oh." I frowned. Sam's snide comments and evasive answers were seriously beginning to get on my nerves, but I ignored them. I considered the new information. The fact that China wanted to talk to me was a start anyway. Besides, I had nothing to fear competition-wise from Ryan and Kirk. Not only did they have girlfriends, but they usually behaved like pigs. Of course, they might always turn on the charm for an incredibly attractive girl— not to mention one who wanted to write about them in the school paper.

"Speak of the devil," Sam whispered. She was gazing at someone directly behind me. I heard footsteps approaching. My pulse quickened.

"What's up?" Sam asked in a loud, clear voice. She smiled broadly. "You have a chance to use that line yet?"

There was laughter right beside me—China's laughter. My heart began to rattle like a jackhammer.

"Not yet," she replied. "I've gotta wait for a class that uses maroon books."

I kept my eyes riveted to my plate. I couldn't

bring myself to look at her. I stared at my cold, half-eaten sandwich as if it could somehow advise me what to do next. My feelings of anxiety were over-whelmed only by feelings of disbelief. *I* had made a fool of myself in front of China—but Sam was al-ready sharing private jokes with her.

"Y'all mind if I have a seat?" China asked.

"Fine with me," Sam said. "Miles?"

I shook my head vigorously.

China plopped down in the third chair. "I'm not interrupting anything, am I?" she asked.

The question snapped me out of my stupor. "Not at all," I replied. There was no way I was going to let Sam respond first. There was no telling *what* she would have said, given her present mood.

I smiled at China. She was wearing a cropped white baby tee. I could see her belly button in the shadows under the rim of the table. I forced myself not to look at it. I brought the sandwich to my lips again.

"You know, I'm sorry. I have to go," Sam sud-denly announced. "I just remembered I've got to find Ariel. I'll see you all later." She hopped out of her chair and snatched her tray off the table—but not before she gave me a big, obvious wink.

I almost choked.

Luckily, China happened to be looking at her plate. I whirled and watched Sam as she strolled across the cafeteria floor, looking very pleased with herself. I was suddenly seething with rage. Was she deliberately trying to make me look like a jerk?

People only winked like that in hackneyed, grade-C teen movies. I would never do something that stupid or immature or asinine to *her*. Not once had I ever winked at her in front of those oversized meatheads on the basketball team she'd gone out with.

". . . bringing my own lunch."

"What?" In my silent frenzy, I hadn't even realized that China was talking to me. "Sorry," I mumbled, putting my sandwich down. I turned to face her. "What were you saying?"

She smiled. "Nothing. I was just saying how I should start bringing my own lunch." She wrinkled her nose in distaste, then pushed the tray away from her. "I forgot how bad the food was."

"I know what you mean." I looked at my own plate. "You know, to tell you the truth, I don't even know what I'm eating."

"The *other* gray meat?" she suggested.

I laughed once. "That sounds like something Sam would say," I said. I instantly hated myself for having said it. Making the connection to Sam had been an unfortunate reflex. I vowed right then and there never to bring up Sam's name in China's presence again.

"As a matter of fact, it is." She shrugged. "But I've been stealing her lines for years."

"Yeah, she told me," I grumbled.

"She did?" China smiled hopefully. "Did she also mention that my story would be a dismal failure if I didn't get to talk to you?"

I laughed again. "Well, not in so many words," I

said, and for the first time since I had met her, I began to relax in her presence. Something about the easy, genuine way she spoke was just so . . . un-intimidating. I couldn't help but feel right at home.

"I hope I'll be able to talk to all three of you guys at the same time—I mean, if that's cool," she said. She tilted her head, twirling her braid with her finger. "I was thinking about stopping by the art studio after school today. I already talked to Kirk Evans about it. Is that all right with you?"

"Sure," I said. *It's perfect, in fact,* I thought. Once she was in the studio, I would be able to study her while I sculpted. Although, on second thought, that might not be such a great idea. She might think I was some kind of crazed stalker or something if she knew I was sculpting her.

"You think Mr. Washington would mind?" she asked.

I shook my head. "Nah. Although I should probably warn you that you'll be subjected to non-stop disco."

She giggled. "That's exactly what Kirk said."

"Did Kirk also mention that the conversation up there is generally very lame?" I asked.

She shook her head. "No way. I find *that* hard to believe."

"Just wait till you get there," I muttered. "You'll see. Most of what we talk about revolves around fighting for space and spreading false rumors. . . ." My voice trailed off when I noticed her expression had suddenly changed. She was squinting at something across the cafeteria, our conversation clearly forgotten. I shifted in my chair and followed her line of sight. There, at a big table at the other end of the room, was Connor Smith, along with a few other wanna-be rock stars. I instinctively scowled.

"I'm sorry," she apologized softly. "What was that last thing you said?"

I turned back to face her. She was looking down at her lap now, her hair shrouding her eyes. Her soft red lips were curved downward.

"It was, uh, nothing," I said awkwardly. The confident feeling that had enveloped me only seconds earlier was now slipping away. Obviously China wasn't over Connor, and judging from the look on her face, she wasn't going to be over him for a long, long time.

She brushed her hair out of her eyes and glanced up at me. "Hey, I'm sorry. Really. It's just that, uh, I'm kind of going through a rough time right now." She managed a smile. "Occasionally I freak out for no apparent reason."

I shrugged. "That's cool. I never have a good reason when I freak out."

She chuckled sadly. "Really? You don't particularly strike me as the kind of person who would ever freak out." She spoke in a faraway voice, as if I weren't even there. "You seem very even and mellow."

"I do?" I laughed automatically. *Mellow?* If she knew how nervous I'd been about talking to her, she definitely wouldn't have used that word. In fact, she'd probably have been running away from me as fast as she could. "Um, I don't know about that," I said after a few seconds.

Our eyes met. Then she shook her head quickly, as if she was embarrassed. Her hair fell in her face. "Look, I better go," she said under her breath. Her already flushed cheeks turned a fiery red. She jumped up from the table and hurried away. "I'll see you this afternoon, okay?"

I opened my mouth, but she was already halfway across the cafeteria before I could even utter a word. I leaned back in my chair and watched her scurry out the door. She kept her head down. She didn't even so much as glance in any other direction. I turned around and blinked a few times. All of a sudden I found myself sitting at an empty table. She hadn't even taken her tray with her.

Why had she bolted so fast?

"You seem very even and mellow."

Her comment echoed through my head. A nervous excitement began to flutter in my stomach. She'd bolted because she was embarrassed. She'd blushed after speaking the words, which meant that she had obviously admitted something to me, something she wished she hadn't. And it was something that she liked.

I smiled.

Maybe, just maybe, she would get over Conner sooner rather than later.

SEVEN

Sam

"**D**O YOU THINK Coach Manigault is on steroids or something?" I groaned. "I feel like I'm in training for the Olympics."

I was sprawled out in the backseat of Ariel's Jeep, staring at the back of her head as she drove me home after practice. Ariel had gotten her voluptuous black hair cut short over the summer, and while the new style looked very glamorous during the school day, it always ended up looking matted and unkempt by the time she was done with her postpractice shower. But she needed to look like a mess every now and then, in my opinion. Ariel Conrad had a perfect body—five feet eleven inches, not an ounce of fat—and a zitless ivory face. People often mistook her for a model. And yes, I was envious of her.

"She's gotta be on *something*," Ariel drawled. "I mean, did you hear her yelling at me at the end

66

of practice? How did she expect me to play when I couldn't even stand?"

"I know. It was totally over the top." I lowered my voice, imitating Coach Manigault. "'Come on, Conrad, let's see some hustle out there! Post up! Set a pick! Now go to the hoop!'"

"I *know*." Ariel laughed miserably. "I was like, 'Gee, Coach, it's kind of hard to do all those things at once, isn't it?'"

I sighed. "Well, I'm just glad it was *you* and not me."

"Thanks a lot, Sam," Ariel said dryly. "It's nice to know you're looking out for me out there."

I laughed, thinking about the similarity between that remark and what Miles had said the other evening: "*It's nice to know you're behind me on this one.*" It was funny—that one little comment had set in motion a whole bizarre chain of events . I started thinking about what had happened that day: first, meeting China, and then finding out that Miles and I weren't in a fight, in spite of what I'd thought. I couldn't believe how much I'd obsessed about a nonexistent argument.

"Hey, Ariel, can I ask you something?" I said.

"As long as it doesn't have to do with basketball," she moaned. "I don't even want to *think* about basketball."

"It doesn't." I bit my lip. "But it's kind of a weird question."

"That's okay," she said. "I like weird questions."

"Have you ever thought you were in a fight

with someone, and then you found out you weren't in a fight with that person at all?"

Ariel shot a quick glance at me over her shoulder. "Uh-oh," she said. "I think exhaustion is making you delirious."

"No, seriously. Let me put it this way." I thought for a second. "Have you ever thought that someone was mad at you when they weren't?"

"Have I ever thought someone was mad at me . . ." Her voice trailed off. "I don't know. Why? You think someone is mad at you?"

"Not exactly." I gazed out the window at the treetops as we passed, debating whether I should even bother pursuing this conversation any further. After all, Miles and I *weren't* in a fight—and that was the important thing. But I was still a little perturbed by the whole scene that day at lunch. For the first time ever, I felt as if the invisible connection between our two brains had been temporarily severed. I'd had no idea what he'd been thinking.

"Oh, it's nothing," I said finally. "It's stupid."

"Well, I'm glad I could be of help." She turned onto my street and slowed to a stop in front of my house, then turned around and gave me an ironic smile. "Anytime you want to talk about something, I'm here for you."

"Ha, ha, ha," I said flatly—but I managed a smile too. I sat up straight and grabbed my book bag, then hopped out of the Jeep. "Thanks for the ride." I closed the door. "See you tomorrow."

She hesitated a moment, looking at me through

the open window. "Hey, Sam, are you sure you're all right?" she asked. "I mean, really?"

I nodded. "Yeah. You know, except for the fact that I might drop dead at any second."

She laughed. "I hear ya. I'll see you tomorrow. Get some rest, huh?" She put the Jeep in gear and pulled away from the curb.

"You too," I called after her.

I paused for a moment under the dark canopy of trees, watching Ariel's Jeep disappear down the deserted street. All at once, an inexplicable gloom settled over me. *Was* I all right? Standing there by myself in my faded jeans and T-shirt, my hair still damp from the shower, I wasn't so sure. I suddenly felt incredibly lonely, as if I were the last person left in the world. Everything looked empty and gray in the fading sunlight. The row of cozy frame houses that stretched endlessly in either direction—houses that were as familiar to me as my own reflection— seemed oddly distant and lifeless. Even my own home looked cold.

I shook my head and began walking across the lawn. I just had a serious case of the back-to-school blues; that was all. And being run ragged on a basketball court for three hours didn't help.

"Hello!" I yelled as I pushed open the front door. I turned on the front hall light. *That* was better. The soft glow made everything seem warmer somehow.

"Hi, Sam," my mom called from the kitchen. "How was your day, honey?"

"Way too long," I replied, climbing the stairs. "Coach Manigault is bent on turning us all into superstars."

"Dinner in fifteen minutes, okay?"

"Okay." Once again I staggered into my room and collapsed onto my bed. I'd done the same thing every afternoon that week. I had the terrible feeling that I would be doing the same thing every afternoon until Christmas.

There was a knock on my door.

"Go away, Beth," I croaked.

"Your boyfriend called, butt-munch," she replied.

If I hadn't been so tired, I might have laughed. Good old Beth. She never changed. I reached for the phone and punched in Miles's number.

"Don't hog the phone," she ordered. Her footsteps pattered away from my door.

I rolled my eyes. "Thanks, *Mom,*" I called after her.

After two rings Miles picked up. "Hello?"

"Hey," I said, sitting up against the pillows. "What's up?"

"What were you thinking today at lunch?" he barked.

I looked at the phone for a second. Well. That was certainly an interesting way of greeting one's best friend. I had been expecting something more along the lines of "Hi, Sam! What's up with you?" Or maybe just "Not much." Something that a normal person would say under normal circumstances.

So I figured the best thing to do would be just to ignore the response he had given and insert a new one of my choosing.

"I'm fine, thanks, Miles," I said. "Nice of you to ask."

"You're not being funny, Sam," he growled. "What were you trying to prove with that stupid wink?"

I frowned. "You want to start from the top, Miles? You'll have to excuse me. I've just had three hours of basketball practice. I'm a little slow right now."

"Today at lunch, when you got up and left, you winked at me. In front of China."

I nearly laughed. "You're mad about *that?*"

"You're damn right I am. I mean, were you trying to make me look bad? Or did you just want to ruin any chance I have with her?"

I couldn't believe what I was hearing. Miles had gone off the deep end. Not only that, he was acting like a total jerk. I took a deep breath, trying to remain calm. "Miles, I was *joking*. She wasn't *looking*. Believe me, I have better things to do with my time than try to ruin your chances with China."

He didn't say anything.

"Look, the whole reason I got up and left was so you could be alone with her!" I shouted.

"Could have fooled me," he muttered.

My eyebrows twisted into a tight, angry knot. Where did he get off talking to me like that? I felt a serious urge to just slam the phone down on the hook right then. "You know, Miles, if it weren't for me, she never would have come over to that table in the first place," I snapped. "*I'm* the one who convinced her that the reason you made a fool out of yourself was because you were pathologically shy."

He didn't respond.

"Miles?"

"Okay, okay," he said grudgingly.

"I'm also the one who told her I would put the two of you in touch, in case you forgot."

"All *right*," he said, with a little more force. "I'm sorry."

"Good." I ran a hand through my moist hair, struggling to relax. For about the fifth time in three days, I felt as if the world had turned upside down. Nothing made sense. Before, I'd thought I was in a fight with Miles and I wasn't; now, for some reason, I *was*. It was ludicrous.

"I'm sorry," he repeated. "Really."

I sighed. "Listen, can we *please* not talk about this anymore? I'm too tired. It's boring. I *want* you to go out with China Henry. I want you two to fall in love, get married, have seventeen babies, and start your own commune. All right? You have my full support."

He laughed quietly. "Thanks, Sam. That's a beautiful thought."

"Yeah, well, whatever." I slouched deep into the pillows. "So how was the rest of your day anyway?"

"Well, now that you mention it, it was actually

pretty good." His voice brightened. "China stopped by the studio."

"Congratulations," I said dully. "What else?"

"She only stopped by for, like, thirty seconds. But she's going to bring her camera tomorrow and hang out there all afternoon with us. Kirk and Ryan were totally flirting with her the whole time. They told her they were going to . . ."

I stopped listening. But Miles just kept babbling, on and on. Was he deaf or something? I'd just told him I didn't want to talk about China anymore.

"Uh, Miles?" I said, cutting him off. "What *else* happened today?"

"Well . . . the best thing of all was that she told me she's probably going to have a whole separate paragraph for me, because I'm the only sculptor. Can you believe that?" He chuckled, sounding disgustingly pleased with himself. "So that's it, I guess. How was *your* day?"

Uncontrollable anger suddenly surged through my veins. Obviously that wink hadn't caused any problems. I *knew* it wouldn't have. It hadn't meant a damn thing. So why had he shouted at me? Was he deliberately trying to make me feel like crap?

"Sam?" he prompted.

"Well, my day was just about perfect, Miles," I said with as much sarcasm as I could muster. "I made a fool of myself in American lit. Coach Manigault tried to give me cardiac arrest. Then I came home and you yelled in my ear. I also made a great new friend. Her name is China Henry!" My

73

voice rose to a giddy, high-pitched shriek. "Maybe she'll ask me to be the maid of honor at your wedding!"

There was silence on the other end.

I just sat there, breathing through clenched teeth. My knuckles turned white as I gripped the phone.

Finally Miles cleared his throat. "Hey, Sam, are you all right?"

"Aagh!" I screamed. "Miles, do you realize that in the six years I've known you, that is possibly the dumbest question you've ever asked?"

There was another pause. "So what's wrong?"

I shook my head. "Look, just forget it. I should really go. Dinner's almost ready. I'll see you tomorrow, all right?"

"Okay," he said hesitantly. "You sure?"

"Good-bye, Miles." I dropped the phone on the hook. There was simply no use talking to him. Not only had the invisible connection between our two brains been severed, it had been zapped right out of existence.

EIGHT

MILES

THURSDAY AFTERNOON I found myself kneeling in front of yet another shapeless lump of clay. I'd started from scratch every single day so far. Each time I opened the refrigerator door and took a look at the previous day's work, I'd notice about a hundred faults. I was seriously considering giving up trying to sculpt China altogether. It was too frustrating. Besides, she *was* going to be in the studio all afternoon, watching me.

"Hey, I think y'all should let me do all the talking when that girl gets here," Kirk announced. "No offense or anything. You know, I'm just worried you might embarrass yourselves."

I glanced up at him. He was pretending to study his canvas, but he was smiling broadly.

"I don't know if that's such a good idea, man," Ryan said, painting a few quick strokes on his own canvas with a thick brush. "I mean, not to be rude or anything, but you obviously forgot your breath mints. And this room is kinda small, if you get my drift."

I groaned inwardly. For the first time all day, I actually began to get a little nervous. I had an awful suspicion that Ryan and Kirk were going to act like complete idiots in front of China and that I would end up looking like an idiot by association.

The door suddenly opened. I jumped slightly, but it was only Mr. Washington. He looked at me and shook his head. "You're starting over *again*, Miles?" he asked. "I think your perfectionism is getting the best of you."

"It's not perfectionism," Kirk said. "It's guilt."

I frowned. "Guilt?"

"That's right." Kirk leaned forward and began painting. "See, I got it all figured out. Every day you work on sculpting this beautiful girl that you supposedly 'made up.' But the next day you come in here, you look at the sculpture, and you're wracked with guilt because you think of poor Samantha Scott, who has no idea that you're unfaithful." He paused. "So you destroy the sculpture and start all over, hoping that you'll forget about this other girl and move on to something completely different."

Mr. Washington looked at me.

"He forgot to take his medicine," I mouthed silently.

"But somehow you end up sculpting her face all over again," Kirk went on. He waved his paintbrush at me dramatically. "You can't help yourself, man. It's like one of those Greek tragedies or something. You're cursed to sculpt your secret girlfriend's face for all eternity, just like that guy who had to roll the boulder up the hill . . . you know . . ." He snapped his fingers.

"Sisyphus?" Mr. Washington prompted.

"Exactly!" Kirk exclaimed. He held his hands to the ceiling. "It's tragic and crazed and twisted—just like . . . what's–his–face."

I began clapping. Ryan immediately joined in.

"That was incredible, man," I said. "You moved me."

"Me too," Ryan agreed. "I mean, that was *deep,* kid."

Kirk held up his hands. "No, no, stop. You're too kind."

Mr. Washington just stared at us, looking mildly concerned. "You know, you're a lot like Larry, Moe, and Curly. The only difference is that you could use some professional help."

I shifted my position, turning my back on Kirk and Ryan. "Yeah. Kirk could definitely use some help. Or maybe he should just give up painting and become a writer." I took the clay in my hands and began rolling it into a ball. "He's great at making stuff up."

"Yeah, well, the truth always hurts, Miles," he said.

I laughed. There was about as much truth to the idea of my thinking about "poor Samantha Scott" as there was to the idea of Elvis being alive and well and living in Austin. I was still pretty angry at Sam, as a matter of fact. *She* was the one who needed help. She had become seriously unbalanced or something in the past few days. One second she was trying to make me look like a fool; then, when *I* apologized to *her,* she turned around and yelled at *me.* And that day at lunch she had completely blown me off without even saying so much as a word. She'd just marched away from our table the moment I sat down. I'd said I was sorry, hadn't I? What more did she expect?

Well, there was no point worrying about it. China would be there any minute. I had to shut Sam out of my mind. I began to knead the clay. Then I heard the ominous sound of Mr. Washington sifting through the crate of tapes.

"Hey, uh, Mr. Washington?" I said. "Maybe just this *one* time, you know—since we're having a guest—do you think we can skip the tunes? You know, she's gonna want to ask us questions and stuff."

"Nice try, Miles," he replied. "*You're* a guest too, you know. And if you can take it, I'm sure she can take it as well." He slipped a tape into the box. I cringed when I heard the familiar strains of some high-pitched male voice singing over seventies elevator music.

"Mr. Washington, have you ever noticed that all the stuff you listen to sounds like it was recorded underwater?" Ryan asked. "You know, all muffled?"

"Is that so, Mr. Lee? It's funny. The music *you* kids listen to sounds a lot like a city being firebombed."

There was a knock on the door.

"Come in," Mr. Washington called.

A brief, jittery warmth washed over me. I instantly forgot about the music, the conversation—*everything*. The moment had arrived.

"Hey," China said, stepping into the room. She gave us all a big smile.

"Welcome," Kirk said. His voice assumed a deep, husky quality. He was probably trying to sound manly, but he sounded more like a game-show host. *Please,* I thought.

"How's it going?" Ryan asked.

"Pretty good," she said.

It was my turn. But I didn't say anything. I just stared at her. I couldn't help it. Every outfit she wore was sexier than the last. That day she was wearing a short, swingy dress with little brown flowers printed on it—flowers that perfectly complemented her chestnut hair. A camera hung around her neck. Her dress actually reminded me of the kind of dress Sam liked to wear.

I frowned. I was *not* going to think about Sam.

All of a sudden China froze. "Oh, my gosh," she murmured. "Are y'all listening to *Superfly?*" She started laughing. "I *love* Curtis Mayfield!"

"You do?" Mr. Washington asked, sounding shocked.

"Totally. It's all I listened to when I was growing up."

"Well, well." Mr. Washington nodded approvingly. Then he gave Kirk, Ryan, and me a triumphant smile. "You know, I thought I'd never live to see the day when someone who actually has decent taste walked in here."

I shook my head. It was unbelievable. China actually *liked* this stuff. Of course, if China liked it, maybe Mr. Washington had been right about the finer things after all.

She gently tapped a finger on her camera in time to the music. "My dad loves this album," she said. "Curtis Mayfield is his favorite. Him and Isaac Hayes. And the Isley Brothers."

"Really?" Mr. Washington laughed out loud. He pointed at the crate of tapes. "You know, I've got plenty of Isaac Hayes and Isley Brothers right here." He glanced at us again. "Feel free to put on whatever you want."

A collective groan rose from Kirk and Ryan, but China didn't seem to notice. She rushed over and began busily pawing through the tapes.

"Oh, *man!*" she cried after a few seconds. She grabbed a cassette and held it up in front of us. "Earth, Wind, and Fire!"

Kirk and Ryan started cracking up. But I was still too entranced even to react. She looked so cute and excited—like a little kid. I felt as if I knew right then that there was much more to her than her looks. For the first time, I felt as if I could *really* fall in love with her as a person.

"Sorry," she said, blushing. "I guess I get a little

carried away sometimes." She dropped the tape back into the crate.

"No need to apologize," Mr. Washington said. He cocked an eyebrow at Kirk and Ryan, then sat on a stool by the door. "You'll have to forgive these boys' rudeness. They *are* decent painters, even if they have no manners."

"Well, I'm the one who's imposing." She hesitated. "So do you mind if I just take a look around and ask some questions? It won't take very long. I mean, I don't want to be in your way."

"You won't be in *my* way," I said. "Kirk and Ryan have already taken care of that."

She smiled at me across the little room, then lifted her camera. A flash suddenly went off in my face. I shook my head and blinked. Little purple spots danced in front of my eyes.

"Sorry. I'm just gonna take a few pictures." She snaked her way through the two easels and stood next to me. "So why do the painters get most of the space anyway?"

"It's like Mr. Washington said," I replied, blinking a few more times. "They're the rudest."

"Don't listen to a word he says," Kirk muttered. "Sculptors are notorious liars. They've done studies. We've even conducted a study in here."

Uh-oh. For a terrible moment I was afraid Kirk was going to bring up his theory of how I lied about my relationship with Sam.

But he didn't. And China wasn't even looking at him. She was looking at me. She was so close that I could hear her breathing softly. I involuntarily tensed.

"So what are you working on?" she asked, leaning over the clay table.

I gazed down at my sorry little gray blob. Kirk and Ryan already had half-finished paintings—and I had *this*. "Uh . . . I *was* working on a bust," I mumbled, feeling very inadequate. "But I kept having to start over."

"Miles is a perfectionist," Mr. Washington interjected.

"Is that true?" She glanced back at him over her shoulder. "I'd love to see something finished." She turned and looked at me again. "I mean, if you have anything here I could see."

I bit my lip. "Uh . . . I don't know." There *were* a couple of old pieces of mine lying around in the studio, but they were so, well, amateurish.

"I bet I could dig up something," Mr. Washington said. He hopped off the stool and headed straight for the smock closet. There, on a shelf above the hangers, was a piece I'd done in the spring: a little goblin about six inches tall with horns and big fangs, playing a banjo. It had a fat stomach and a silly grin and a forked tongue sticking out of its mouth.

I wrung my hands together, feeling anxious. The piece looked infantile to me now, like a discarded toy. I hadn't even painted or glazed it. Mr. Washington gingerly lifted it off the shelf and placed it before China on the clay table.

"*You* did this?" she exclaimed.

"Uh-huh," I muttered reluctantly.

She bent down and studied it closely, her eyes wide. She giggled. "This is so cool. I mean, it's so funny. What do you call it?"

"What do I *call* it?" My face became hot. "I, uh, never really thought about it."

I shot a quick glance at Kirk and Ryan. Both of them had stopped painting. They were staring at me with curious, puzzled smiles. I swallowed. They were starting to make me nervous. Had they made the connection between the bust I'd been sculpting and China? It seemed like a long shot, but still . . .

"Can I have it?" China asked.

I turned back to face her. She was looking up at me eagerly.

"You really want it?" I asked, not quite able to believe her.

She nodded.

"Okay," I said slowly. "But you know . . . I could make you something else." The words seem to fall out of my mouth even before I knew what I was saying. "I could sculpt, you know, a bust of you. I mean, like your head or something." My lips clamped shut. How stupid had *that* sounded?

"Really?" she asked excitedly. "Oh, wow. That would be awesome, Miles."

I just stood there, at a complete loss for words. *Miles.* It was the first time she had ever called me by name.

"You know, I could paint a picture of you

too," Kirk cut in. "I'm the portrait artist here."

Without thinking, I glared at him. But his grin just widened.

"Sure," China said. She strolled over to Kirk's canvas and took a look at it. Then she laughed. "Hey, that's Mr. Washington!"

Instinctively I walked over to Kirk's easel and took a look too. I'd been so absorbed in my own work all week that I hadn't even really noticed what Kirk was working on. But sure enough, there was Mr. Washington, painted to look about twenty years younger, with a big afro and a wide-collared paisley shirt. He was wearing sunglasses. The shades of gray, black, and white Kirk had used gave the portrait a grainy, antique quality, like an old photograph. I shook my head.

"That is killer, man," I murmured. "I mean, that is really, really good."

Kirk shrugged. "Thanks. I wanted to capture him at a time when people actually *listened* to the music he cruelly forces on us."

Mr. Washington smirked, but he was nodding admiringly. "It's really not bad. Aside from the fact that my hair *never* looked like that." He sat back down on the stool. "You better let me take that one home, Mr. Evans. I don't know if it's appropriate to keep on school grounds."

China shook her head. "All this stuff is great. How come you guys have never had an exhibition? I mean, nobody even really knows what you do up here. It's so amazing."

Kirk, Ryan, and I just looked at each other. I was sure they were asking themselves the same question I was. *Amazing?*

"I . . . uh, just never felt ready," I mumbled.

"Well, not that I'm any kind of expert, but *I* think you're ready." She glanced at us. We were all crowded around her now.

"Um . . . you know what?" she said, clearing her throat. "There's so little room in here that I think it might be easier if I talked to each of you somewhere else, one at a time. That way I won't be disturbing you as you work. There's an empty classroom next door." She looked at me. "Miles, you wanna go first?"

I nodded, trying my best to act casual. "Sure."

"Great." She headed for the door. "As soon as I'm done with Miles, I'll send him back in here to get someone else."

I followed her out into the hall, feeling more elated with each passing second. This was going even better than I had expected. I was actually going to be alone with her, one-on-one.

"Go easy on him," Kirk called after us. "He's very fragile—"

I shut the door behind us before he could get another word out. Then I smiled at her. "Kirk has a hard time shutting up sometimes. It's a good thing I'm going first."

She laughed. "He *does* seem like kind of a talker. I think I'll save him for last."

I hesitated, waiting for her to lead the way. "So, uh . . ."

She pointed to an open classroom door—the door to the same classroom, in fact, where she'd had her fight with Connor. I wondered if it was going to bring back any memories. "Let's use that one," she said.

I nodded. "Sounds cool."

As we approached I heard the very faint sounds of a band coming from behind the big metal door at the end of the hall. The room must have been soundproofed. Was it Connor's band?

As if on cue, Connor Smith appeared at the top of the stairs at the end of the hall, a guitar case slung over his shoulder.

Unconsciously, my fists clenched at my sides.

Both he and China froze when they saw each other. Then Connor's face broke into a wide smile. "China!" he called. He jogged down the hall. "Wow. It's lucky I ran into you."

China's lips pressed into a tight line. "Why's that?" she demanded flatly.

He stopped in front of us. He didn't even seem to notice I was there. He just looked at China. "Well, because I wanted to invite you to a gig tomorrow night."

"*What?*" she snapped. "Are you *serious?*"

"Of course I'm serious." He gently laid his hand on her arm. I resisted the temptation to swat it off. "Look, China, you know, it's not like we have to stop being friends or anything. That kind of thing is so stupid."

I shifted on my feet, suddenly feeling uncomfortable.

Connor was deliberately ignoring me. By talking about their relationship as if I weren't there, he was probably trying to prove in a very lame way that my presence wasn't even worthy of being acknowledged. He was showing me that I meant nothing to him. I couldn't have cared less, but I couldn't help but be embarrassed for China's sake.

China wrenched her arm from his grasp. "Connor, in case you didn't notice, I'm *busy* right now. I'll talk to you later." She brushed past him and headed for the classroom door. "Come on, Miles," she said.

I hesitated. Connor and I were standing side by side now, staring at her.

"Oh, come on, China." He laughed. "You don't need to get all huffy. I just want you to come to the gig on Friday. It's at the Mad Hatter. It's a big one for us. Is that too much to ask?"

"As a matter of fact, it is," she said. "And I'm busy that night anyway."

He laughed again. "Yeah. Right. What are you doing?"

She looked me directly in the eye. "Miles and I have plans."

I blinked. My stomach twisted slightly. What was she thinking? The last thing I wanted was to be caught in the middle of this ridiculous argument. She was obviously lying—just using the first excuse that popped into her head. But she was starting to smile. And even though I was totally flabbergasted—not to mention a little angry—I couldn't help but smile back.

Connor jerked a thumb at me without even bothering to turn his head in my direction. "*Him?* Give me a break, China."

Now I was furious. Who did this guy think he was? I decided right then that even if China *was* lying just to teach him a lesson, I'd be glad to help. "That's right," I said. I marched over and stood beside her.

He still refused to look at me. He was tenacious; I had to give him that. "So what are these *plans* anyway?" he asked, glowering at China.

She shrugged. "We haven't decided yet."

"Whatever they are, seeing your band isn't gonna be a part of them," I said calmly.

"I didn't ask *you,*" he barked. "I wasn't talking to you."

"That's okay," I replied. "I wasn't talking to *you* when I told China that I think your band sucks."

I half expected him to lunge at me. But instead, he just shook his head, smiling that cocky smile of his. "Dude, don't you know that nobody cares what you think?"

I smiled back, trying to think of some devastatingly witty comeback, but before I could, China grabbed my arm and yanked me into the classroom. "*I* care what he thinks," she stated. "I'll talk to you later, Connor." And with that, she slammed the classroom door so hard that it rattled in its frame.

For what seemed like a very long time, we just stood by the door in that empty classroom, staring at each other. Neither of us moved. Neither of us even seemed to be breathing. Finally I heard the sounds of Connor's footsteps walking back down the hall.

China sighed deeply. She smiled, and I smiled back. I was expecting her to thank me for bailing her out of a touchy situation. I was also sort of expecting her to proceed with the interview, as if nothing had happened. I was expecting a lot of things—except for what she actually said.

Which was this: "So, Miles. What do you feel like doing tomorrow night?"

NINE
SAM

THE LAST KERNEL of popcorn posed a little bit of a problem. My stomach had reached critical mass. It was on the verge of a major explosion. But I managed to put the piece of popcorn in my mouth. I chewed the cold, salty, greasy thing and forced it down. Then I set the huge bowl on the glass coffee table and stretched out across the living room couch.

I was hoping to feel at least some satisfaction from the heroic accomplishment of eating more popcorn than humanly possible—but no. Contrary to my expectations, skipping basketball practice and stuffing my face like a trash compactor was *not* the miracle cure for depression. I felt just as mopey and miserable as I had before. The only difference was that I now felt totally ill as well.

"What is my problem?" I asked out loud. My question echoed off the walls of the empty house.

Maybe I should have gone to practice. Even Coach Manigault's form of cruel and unusual punishment was better than *this*.

I fumbled for the remote control and turned on the TV. For a while I flipped listlessly through the channels, but between the news and *Home Improvement* reruns, there was nothing on. Finally I gave up and settled once again for total silence. The remote fell to the rug with an unceremonious thump.

The worst part about the whole situation was that I had no idea *why* I was so upset. I knew when it had started, though—the day before, when Ariel asked me if I was all right. As soon as somebody asks you if you're all right, you always know that you aren't.

The phone rang. It had rung once before. I still had no desire to pick it up. The first call had been from Miles. He'd left a message insisting that I call him back as soon as possible—but I had no desire to do that either. I had no desire to do anything. I waited for the machine to pick up, but it didn't. After four rings, there was nothing. The person must have hung up. Good.

I was almost certain it had been Miles again.

Miles, Miles, Miles, I thought disgustedly. *Why do I always end up thinking about Miles? It's not as if he's the cause of all my problems.*

No. He wasn't. I'd reminded myself of *that* little fact maybe a thousand times in the last twenty-four hours.

But at that moment, as I lay there feeling like an overstuffed Christmas roast, I suddenly knew I'd been fooling myself. In the back of my mind, I knew the way I was feeling had *everything* to do with Miles. I was just scared to admit it.

I was scared to admit that I might be drifting away from my best friend.

I rolled over on my side and gazed at the blank TV set. What had gone wrong? From the moment school started, things had gotten inexplicably weird between us. We just couldn't seem to communicate anymore. It was senseless. I'd spent almost every waking moment with him that summer. We'd never been closer. So why was there a problem now, of all times?

Well, a lot of it had to do with his sudden obsession with China; I knew that much. He couldn't seem to talk about anything else. No doubt the message he'd left had something to do with her. And maybe I *was* a little envious of China Henry, even though I hadn't wanted to admit that either. Maybe I was even jealous. But I had the right to be. After all, Miles had never invited *me* up to the studio, and I was his best friend. In fact, the past spring after basketball season, he had actually forbidden me to visit him there. According to him, my presence would have made him and the other guys feel too self-conscious. And China's presence wouldn't? Evidently not. She had been there *twice* already.

I should have never opened my big mouth, I told myself. *I should have told China that Miles wasn't interested in being interviewed at all. I should have—*

My thoughts were scattered by the sound of the front door opening.

"Hello?" Beth called. "Mom?"

I immediately sat up and brushed my hair out of my face, struggling to collect myself. My little sister was standing in the front hall, not ten feet away. She jumped when she noticed me looking at her.

"Jeez!" she shrieked. "You scared me half to death. What are you doing here?"

"Uh . . . I didn't feel like going to basketball practice today," I said lamely.

She took a closer look at me, squinting at me through the shadows. I hadn't realized how dark the house had become. I must have looked like a lunatic, sitting there with all the lights off. "Are you sick or something?" she asked.

I shook my head.

"What's wrong, then?" She grinned. "Miles didn't finally dump you, did he?"

That was it. All the anger, all the frustration, all the pent-up fury swelled up inside me, ready to burst. I wanted to scream, to curse, to tell her in the most obscene way possible to get lost . . . but I couldn't. I opened my mouth, and all that came out was an insignificant little gasp. My voice caught. A large, painful lump had suddenly lodged itself in my throat. I blinked, then turned away.

"Hey, uh, Sam?" Beth murmured. She took a few steps toward me. "Seriously, are you all right? What's the matter?"

"Nothing," I whispered hoarsely. I tried to swallow. I couldn't believe I was about to cry; it was totally preposterous. I must have been losing my mind. "I just want to be alone, all right?"

"You know, Sam, you *can* talk to me about stuff," she said. "I'm thirteen now. I'm not a little kid anymore. I can handle it."

I drew in a deep, quivering breath. "It's nothing," I insisted. "Really."

Beth didn't say anything for a few seconds. Then she blurted, "Have you ever noticed that you have this shell around you?"

"Oh, jeez," I moaned. This was perfect. Now my little sister was psychoanalyzing me. That was *exactly* what I needed. "Beth, please—"

"I'm serious. You always try to come across like this tough jock chick. But it doesn't always work. Maybe you should let your guard down once in a while."

"Beth, that has nothing to do with *anything!*" I cried.

Just then the doorbell rang. *Now what?* I thought wretchedly. Given my luck, it was probably Ariel, coming to yell at me about how I had let the team down.

"Who is it?" Beth called.

"Miles," came the muted reply. "Is Sam there?"

I whirled around again.

Beth was looking at me apprehensively, waiting for me to make the decision as to whether I was here or not. My mind raced. Did I want to deal with Miles right now? My breath started coming quickly. I rubbed my hands on my jeans and found that my palms were moist. But then I thought: *Why am I freaking out?* Of course he could come in. Then we could finally get everything out in the open and clear this mess up once and for all.

I nodded.

Beth shrugged, then opened the door. "Hey," she said.

"Is she here?" he asked urgently.

"Uh . . . yeah." She stepped aside.

Miles burst into the hall, then sighed when he saw me. "Whew. Are you all right?"

"Yeah," I replied, a little taken aback. "Why?"

"Well, it's just that I looked for you in the gym today—you know, when I was done in the studio. But Ariel said you were home sick." He flopped down beside me on the couch and smiled in the dim half-light. "Then when I called, there was no answer. I guess I got a little worried. Even though I shouldn't have been. I *am* mad at you."

"Mad at me?" The lump in my throat began to subside. "Why's that?"

He raised his eyebrows. "Well, you *did* hang up on me the other night. . . ." His smile widened. "Do you have this weird feeling of déjà vu? Didn't we already have this conversation?"

"Yeah." I laughed softly. "I guess we did."

"So what's up? *Are* you sick?"

I glanced at Beth, who was still standing in the front hall, staring at us. "Um, do you mind?" I asked.

Her mouth fell open. "Well, excuse me for living," she hissed. Then she stomped loudly up the stairs and slammed the door to her room. For a second I felt bad. After all, she *had* been concerned. *Oh, well,* I thought. *I'll make it up to her later.*

"I, uh, didn't feel like going to practice today," I said after a moment.

He peered at me closely. The soft curve of his cheekbone was silhouetted against the light from the hall. "You aren't thinking about quitting the team, are you?"

I shook my head. "No. I just needed a rest."

"Hmmm." He nodded thoughtfully, then brushed a lone strand of hair out of his face. His gaze flickered over me. "Coach Manigault is really bringing you down, huh?"

"Coach Manigault?" I asked. My face fell. How could he be so clueless? "Miles, this has nothing to do with basketball."

"It doesn't?" He shifted on the sofa. The reflection of the front hall light now glistened in his brown eyes like two twinkling stars. "So what is it? Why have you been acting so weird all of a sudden?"

"Me?" I cried. "What about *you?*"

He leaned back, looking genuinely stunned. "How have *I* been acting weird?"

"Miles, you—you've become this totally sniveling, spineless, pining little . . . little *wuss*," I stammered, too agitated to form a coherent thought.

"Whoa." He sat up straight. "You wanna run that by me again?"

"China Henry has turned your brain to slop!" I yelled.

"China Henry?" His eyes narrowed. "Sam, you're not making any sense. I thought you *liked* China. I thought you wanted us to get married and have seventeen babies and——"

"Stop it," I interrupted. "Look, I have nothing against China. The only thing I have against *anything* is that you haven't been yourself since you met her."

"I haven't been myself," he repeated flatly. Then he stood up and began pacing around the room. "You know, maybe I should just get out of here," he mumbled. "You're obviously pissed off about *something*. You're using this China thing as an excuse. So I doubt if you're in the mood to hear what I came to tell you."

"Came to *tell* me?" I asked. "Is that why you're here—to tell me something?" Now I was majorly offended. "I thought you were here because you were worried."

"Whatever, Sam," he breathed. "Look. Just forget it."

I shook my head violently. "No way. You brought it up. What did you come here to tell me?"

He stopped pacing. "You really want to know?"

"Yup." I folded my arms across my chest. My heart was pounding. "I really want to know."

"Fine. China and I are going out tomorrow night."

I froze, processing the words. China and Miles

had a date. My insides felt curiously empty, as if all the popcorn I had eaten had magically evaporated. In its place there was a diseased feeling, gnawing at me. But I ignored it. It meant nothing. I leaned forward until I was perched precariously on the edge of the couch. "You came all the way over here to tell me that?" I asked in a hollow voice.

He hesitated, then began walking around the room again. "Well, I actually wanted to ask your advice about something," he said.

"Fine," I replied bitterly. "Don't pinch her butt on the first date."

He glared at me. Then he headed straight for the door. "I should have known better," he muttered under his breath.

"Miles," I called after him—and before I knew it, I was hopping up and chasing him into the front hall. I couldn't let him go like that. I felt sick. Being nasty hadn't made me feel any better; it had only made me feel worse. "Look, I'm sorry," I whispered, placing myself between him and the door. "That was uncalled-for. Tell me what you wanted to tell me. I mean it."

He just reached past me for the doorknob. "Sam, I can't talk to you when you're like—"

"Miles, I'm sorry." My voice was pleading now, but I couldn't help it. I *had* to make him stay. "Please. I—I don't know what's wrong. Just talk to me."

His jaw remained tightly set, but his hand eventually fell to his side. "Look. It's no big deal. It's just that China only asked me out because we ran into her ex-boyfriend. He wanted her to go to some gig of his, and so on the spur of the moment she made up this lie about how she had plans with me."

Relief flooded through me. So it *wasn't* an actual date. It was a scheme on China's part, and Miles happened to be the unfortunate victim. He obviously wouldn't follow through with any of it. "So what did you say?" I asked.

He shrugged. "Well, that's the thing. We actually went ahead and made plans to see a movie. I'm going to meet her at the Guadalupe Street Theater at quarter to eight on Friday night."

I waited. There had to be something else he wasn't telling me. I studied his face, but I couldn't seem to read his expression. "Uh . . . you aren't planning on actually going, are you?" I asked.

"Of course I am," he said. "Why wouldn't I?"

"Because she's *using* you, Miles. You said it yourself. The whole thing was a lie. She's using you to get back at her ex-boyfriend. She probably won't even be there."

"What makes you think that?" His voice rose slightly.

"Miles, she's not interested in you!" I shouted.

His eyes smoldered. I'd never seen him look so angry in his life. "You'd love that, wouldn't you?" he spat. "You'd love it if she wasn't interested. You know, I don't think it's ever occurred to you to actually say something nice or complimentary to anyone in your whole life. I'm not attractive enough, right? I'm not cool enough for her. She's out of my league. Just go ahead and tell me."

"That's not what I'm saying." My voice was quavering. His words stung as sharply as if I had been slapped, but I refused to show any kind of reaction. "I'm just telling you what I *think,* Miles. I'm being honest. You said you wanted my advice. I'm giving it to you. *Don't* go on that date."

"Why not? Because I might actually have a good time? Just forget it, Sam." He shoved me aside and threw the door open, then stormed out into the evening twilight.

"What do you want me to say?" I screamed. "How do you think I feel? You did the same thing to me! When you acted so shocked that she thought we were going out—that was *your* way of telling me that I'm not attractive enough . . ."

But he had already vanished around the corner.

My entire body was shaking. I leaned against the door frame. My breath came in shuddering gasps. Still, as painful as it was, I silently forced myself to finish the sentence I had started: *That was your way of telling me that I'm not attractive enough . . . to be your girlfriend.*

Of course.

I knew then that a terrible truth had finally revealed itself to me, one that was at the root of all my despair. Everything fell into place. Everything made sense—the confusion, the sadness, the torment, the desperate hope that China hadn't been interested . . . even the shell that my sister had been talking about. They were all symptoms of the same, all-consuming sickness.

I was in love with Miles.

What have I done? I asked myself feverishly. *What have I done?*

Somehow, I'd been wrong all along. I hadn't drifted away from my best friend; I'd fallen in love with him. There was no other logical or reasonable explanation. And there was nothing that I could possibly do or say to fix the situation. There never would be. I had most likely ruined whatever relationship we had left. I'd denied the truth to myself for so long that I'd let him get away—I'd even *helped* him find someone else. He wouldn't be coming back. Not now, and probably not ever.

I'd lost him.

After one last hopeless glance into the darkness, I shut the door. It was only then that the tears started flowing freely down my cheeks.

TEN

MILES

WHEN I SAW the glowing numbers on my watch change from 8:04 to 8:05, the nervous pit in my stomach expanded. I had upgraded from anxiety to mild panic.

China was now officially twenty minutes late.

I glanced in both directions down Guadalupe. There was still no sign of her. All I saw was the familiar stream of faceless passersby. I'd been standing outside the theater since seven-forty, and now I was all alone. The movie was supposed to start at eight; everybody else was inside. By now the previews were probably over. I *hated* being late for movies. I also hated standing on a busy street by myself, obviously waiting for somebody and looking like a total loser.

Maybe Sam was right, I thought. *Maybe the whole thing was a lie.*

I took a ten-dollar bill out of my pants pocket

and fidgeted with it. At least I would save the eight bucks for the price of a ticket. A cool breeze rustled my hair. I shivered. For the first time I really felt as if autumn had arrived—and it only served to enhance my grim mood. I'd give China five more minutes, I decided, and then I'd take off.

But no, I knew I wouldn't. There *had* to be some sort of reasonable explanation. I doggedly refused to believe I had been stood up. Of course, I hadn't confirmed the date with China at school that day. I hadn't even seen her. I hadn't called her either. I didn't even know her *number*. But the day before, she had seemed so psyched. . . .

I crumpled the bill with my fingers. I was too keyed up to stand still. It was all Sam's fault. I wouldn't have had any doubts about China if I hadn't gone over to Sam's house. *Sam* was the one who had single-handedly destroyed my self-confidence. *Sam* was the one who was making me miserable right now.

And the pitiful thing was, I still felt guilty.

The previous night, after I had stormed off, I'd been completely miserable. I'd gone home and relived the fight over and over in my mind, trying to figure out the precise moment things had gone so wrong between us. We'd *never* fought like that before, not in six years of being best friends. I knew I was partially to blame. I'd been way too harsh with her when I'd told her that she'd never said a nice thing to anyone in her life. That wasn't true at all. She always told me that I was the most talented sculptor in the world, and that I was a fool for not telling anyone about it. I smiled sadly. That sentiment was deluded but pretty damn flattering nonetheless.

But still, she was much more responsible for the rift between us than I was. Something was bothering her—something big—and she was keeping it hidden. I couldn't help her if she didn't want to talk about it. She was just using China Henry as an excuse to vent her anger. If she couldn't trust her best friend, then she couldn't trust—

"Miles!"

China. I looked up, instantaneously elated. China was running toward me, shaking her head. "Miles, I'm *so* sorry!"

The problem with Sam suddenly seemed very, very far away. And the closer China came, the further Sam drifted from my consciousness. In any case, Sam had been wrong, and that was the important thing. China was here *now*. The long wait was forgotten. She was standing in front of me, smiling and out of breath, looking absolutely beautiful. She wore a short one-piece black dress and a baggy unbuttoned gray sweater. It hung loosely off one shoulder. Her tiny fingertips barely poked out of the sleeves. Her hair was tousled from the run, and her glowing face was radiant.

"I am *so* sorry," she panted. "My dad . . . he *promised* me I could have the car, then he changed his mind at seven-thirty. I was like, 'Dad, I have to be somewhere in fifteen minutes!' He was like,

'Take the bus, dear. That's what it's here for.' So then I was going to call you to tell you I'd be late, but I didn't have your number—"

"China, it's okay." I laughed. "Really."

She sighed, then grinned ruefully. "Well, all right." She glanced at the marquee. "What time is it anyway?"

I glanced at my watch. "Ten past," I said.

"Oh, boy . . ." She shook her head again.

"Don't worry about it. We don't *have* to see a movie."

"I guess you're right." She chewed her lip for a moment. "What do you feel like doing?"

I shrugged.

"Uh, you wanna just walk around or something?" she asked. "It's kind of a nice night."

I nodded. Only moments earlier the fall breeze had seemed like a portent of doom; now it felt crisp and invigorating. "Sounds good."

She sidled up to me as we began walking down Guadalupe in the direction of West Forty-fifth Street. "How long were you waiting?" she asked.

"Not long," I lied. I stared at the sidewalk under my feet. "Maybe fifteen minutes."

"Well, that's not *too* bad." Her arms swung freely at her sides. "The bus is so slow."

I looked at her out of the corner of my eye. "Where do you live anyway?"

"Not far from here, actually. In the south part of Hyde Park."

"Mmm-hmmm. Near that park with the big jungle gym?"

"Yeah!" She spoke in that same excited voice she'd used when she'd found that Earth and Fire tape—or whatever it was—in Mr. Washington's cassette collection. "You know that park? I used to play there all the time when I was a kid."

I smiled. "Me too."

"Hey—maybe we used to play together," she said brightly.

"Yeah, that's what my friend Sam always tries to tell me." The response had come naturally, but after a few more steps I realized what I had just said. My smile vanished. Bringing up Sam's name was becoming a bad habit. Hadn't I sworn to myself that I wouldn't talk about her in China's presence? Besides, I didn't know if she even qualified as a friend anymore.

"Did she also used to play there?" China asked.

I nodded unenthusiastically.

"Maybe I played with her too." She looked up at me and laughed.

"Maybe," I mumbled, trying my best to humor her.

"You know, that girl seriously cracks me up."

I nodded again, but the remark had struck a faintly sour chord within me. I always disliked it when people referred to others as "that girl" or "that guy." It was so . . . well, impersonal, like saying she was an object instead of a human being. Besides, China knew her by name. She wasn't "that girl"—she was Sam.

"How long have you guys been best friends?" China asked.

I almost frowned. But when I looked at her, smiling innocently, I knew she was just trying to make polite conversation. She was sticking to a topic she very reasonably thought I'd enjoy: my best friend. I shrugged, struggling to shake off the bad mood that seemed to be creeping up on me for no apparent reason. "I guess about six years," I said.

"Wow," China said. "That's really cool. I mean, you almost never find people who have been best friends for so long—especially a guy and a girl. You two are one of a kind."

"Yeah. One of a kind."

All at once I stopped. There was a huge window to my right, one that was instantly familiar. We were standing right in front of Phineas Bloom's Vintage Clothing. A strange feeling gripped me, as if I had caught a whiff of some scent, like the smell of homemade cookies, that reminded me of a certain period of my life, far in the past.

"What is it?" China asked.

I didn't answer. I was thinking about what Sam had said on Sunday: "*That guy is probably gonna sell those helmets anyway.*" Although I wasn't quite sure why, I felt it was very important that they still be there. I peered at the glass. The store was dark. I could see only the reflection of China and me on the sidewalk. I took a step forward and pressed my face against the window, cupping my hands around my eyes. Sure enough, both helmets were sitting in the shadows. The pale light of the street lamps glittered dimly in the sparkly paint. I breathed a quick sigh of relief.

"Thinking about buying some vintage clothing?" China asked teasingly.

I shook my head, then turned away from the window. "Uh . . . I'm not sure," I said. Oddly enough, that was the truth. Less than a week earlier I'd been absolutely certain that Sam and I were going to spend the next summer riding around the country together. Now I wasn't even sure if I'd be *talking* to her by then.

"Hey, Miles, are you all right?"

I met her gaze, caught off guard by the question. I was about to tell her that I was fine, but the empathetic look in her eye made me pause. It was as if she understood, somehow, that something was seriously wrong with my life. Was I that transparent? "Oh, it's nothing," I said after a minute. I tried to smile. "Occasionally I freak out for no particular reason. You know what I mean?"

She laughed lightly. "Yeah. I know what you mean."

We resumed our plodding walk. I shoved my hands in my pockets, staring once again at the paved concrete. Without saying a word, she slipped her hand around my left arm.

We stayed for a while just like that, arm in arm, in perfect silence. It was funny. I had expected to feel some sort of magical, electric charge when she touched me—but I didn't. I wasn't sure *how* I felt . . . I only knew it was nice.

"You know, we don't even have to go out tonight if you don't want to," she murmured.

"No," I said quickly. "I want to. I'm sorry. I'm just, uh . . ." I paused, wondering what kind of excuse I should make up. But then I realized there was no real reason to lie about what was going on. In fact, I would probably feel better if I talked about it. And it wasn't as if China was totally removed from the situation; she knew Sam. She *liked* Sam.

I took a deep breath. "Well, you know how you said that it was really cool that Sam and I were still best friends after six years?"

She nodded.

"I don't know if that's true anymore. I don't even know if we're friends at all." I felt as if a dam inside me had broken; the words came flooding out. "We're in a major fight right now. And the thing is, I don't even know how it happened."

China looked up at me. She hesitated, fiddling with her braid with her free hand. "Miles, I'm really sorry," she said quietly. "I had no idea. Did this just happen today or something?"

I shook my head. "No. I didn't even *see* her today. I guess it sort of came to a head last night. But it's been brewing all week long."

She nodded, then looked back down at her feet again. Her grip tightened gently—barely noticeably—around my arm.

"You know, it's funny," I went on, prompted by the reassuring gesture. "Last weekend was, like, the best we'd ever gotten along in our lives. We had all these big plans. Next summer, after graduation, we were going to drive around the country on a motorcycle with a little sidecar. We talked about it for weeks. I mean, we were even going to buy these American-flag motorcycle helmets that they're selling at that vintage clothing store back there and give them to each other for Christmas—"

I suddenly realized that China was staring at me. *Great,* I thought. I had just made a complete fool of myself. "Sorry, I'm rambling," I mumbled. "You don't want to hear this. I'm probably boring you half to death."

"No, no, not at all." She shook her head. "I was just thinking about how incredible that sounds. You guys are so lucky . . . I mean, to have each other as friends." Her voice softened. "None of my friends would ever think to do something like that."

I swallowed. There was something upsetting about what she had just said. I found that I was filled with sadness: for myself, since I'd possibly lost Sam as a friend, and for China, who'd never experienced a friendship like ours. I couldn't believe what was happening to me. It was ridiculous. Why was I even talking about this stuff now? I was on a date with the girl of my dreams. I needed to snap out of it, fast.

"You really have no idea how this fight started?" China asked.

My pace picked up just a little bit. The only thing I was certain of was that the substance of our fight had been over *her.* But there was no way I would tell her that. I had to change the subject.

"I'm sorry, Miles," she said after a minute. "You

don't have to talk about this with me. It's none of my business."

"No, it's not that," I said. I glanced at her. Her head was bent, and her face was slightly concealed by her hair, but I could tell that she was embarrassed, which made me feel even worse. "I like talking about it to you. I feel like I can talk about *anything* to you. It's just that . . . I want us to have a good time, that's all."

She turned and gave me a shy smile. "I *am* having a good time."

I blushed. "Well, uh—I'm glad," I said inanely.

"It's nice to be with someone who doesn't feel the need to hide everything," she added.

I didn't know how to respond to that. It was a compliment, yes—but a strange one. I didn't feel quite as good as I had a moment before.

My thoughts darkened. No, I didn't feel good at all, now that I really thought about it. She had obviously been making a veiled reference to Connor. And I couldn't help but think about what Sam had told me—that the only reason China had made this date was to get back at him. Still, she was *here*, wasn't she? She didn't have to hold on to my arm if she didn't want to. But a terrible, nagging suspicion had planted itself in the back of my mind, and it was growing rapidly. *I'm being used,* I said to myself. Even if *I* didn't feel the need to hide things, maybe China did.

"Hey, China—can I ask you something?" I blurted.

We stopped walking. She looked me in the eye. "Of course," she said.

"You might get offended."

She smiled wryly. "I doubt it."

I glanced down at the ground, debating precisely how to word the question without ruining the night. But I couldn't back down now. Finally I just looked at her and said, "Are you here with me now just to get back at Connor?"

Her smile wavered, but she didn't take her eyes off me. Instead, she took a step back. She slipped her hand out from under my arm and used it to play with her braid. "You really *do* like to get everything out in the open, don't you?"

I lifted my shoulders. "I just want to know," I said. "I mean, it's kind of pointless for us to be doing this if you don't really want to be here in the first place. For the right reasons, I mean."

She lowered her gaze. She opened her mouth, then closed it, then laughed once, very quietly. "You're right. You're totally right. And I guess I *did* want to make him mad, at first. But you want to know the honest truth?" She looked up at me again. "He hasn't crossed my mind once until just now, when you brought him up."

I took a step toward her. We were now standing only inches apart. I wanted to scrutinize every little movement on her face; I wanted to look *into* her—to make sure she was telling the truth. But there was no hint of deception. There was only that perfect, flawless set of features: those red lips and soft cheeks and wild eyes.

"Do you believe me?" she asked. Her voice wasn't much more than a whisper.

I nodded.

"Miles, I don't want to think about Connor anymore," she murmured. "He's part of the past. I had some good times with him, but it's over. To tell you the truth, I was much more scared of not having a boyfriend than I was of losing *him*—if that makes any sense."

"It does," I said. I remembered how I felt when I'd gone out with Jennifer Moreland in the tenth grade. I hadn't even *liked* her. I'd just liked the feeling of knowing that I had a girlfriend.

"But Miles, listen." She brought her face even closer. Her breath nuzzled my chin. "I didn't think I'd be able to forget him so fast. It's weird. I mean . . . you're like a total breath of fresh air to me. You aren't like any of the people I hang out with. You don't care about all the stupid stuff they care about. I mean, when I'm with you, I don't think about that stuff either. I just think about you."

My heart was beating fast, but at the same time I felt remarkably cool. Maybe it was because she had exactly expressed the way I felt about *her*. All the people walking past us, all the bright lights of Guadalupe Street, everything around me just dropped right out of existence. China's face filled my entire field of vision. I felt as if I could be content to stand just like this for the rest of my life.

"Does that make any sense?" she breathed, closer still.

I nodded.

"I'm glad."

And as if acting on their own will, our lips bridged the last gap between us and met in a soft kiss in the cool night air.

ELEVEN
SAM

Friday, 10:05 P.M.

I CAN'T BELIEVE the second week of school has already come and gone. What's even harder to believe is that a full eight days have gone by since I last talked to Miles. Then again, I don't know if talked is the right word. Eight days have gone by since I last screamed at him, or looked him in the eye, or had any sort of communication with him.

I've seen him a few times, of course. Every day at lunch, I see him sitting at our old table. The only difference is that China is there too. So I guess that their date last week must have gone pretty well, despite my dire warnings. I eat with Ariel now. But I'm considering sitting by myself. Yesterday Ariel asked me if Miles was going out with China. I wanted to shove her face into my plate of shepherd's pie.

I guess it's true. Miles really does have a girlfriend. At least, that's what I hear. Nobody's said anything about it to my face. But then again, I'm always the last to hear about these things.

Anyway, today was the worst day of my life, I think. First of all, China (who's been acting way too friendly toward me) asked if she could talk to me after class. She then proceeded to tell me that Miles is "all torn up" about the fact that we're in a fight.

She was telling me about the fight.

So I guess this means that Miles has seen fit to confide in his new best friend, China Henry. He's now talking to her about me behind my back. Let's see. He's known her for less than two weeks, and I've been his closest friend for six years. Is that right? Yes. I just wanted to get that straight.

On a different note, what kind of cheeseball uses an expression like "all torn up"?

I thanked her, though. I was very polite. I very politely told her that if Miles had a problem, he needed to talk to me about it in person. Not through some dizzy go-between. (I left out that last part.) But she said that Miles was nervous about talking to me. I told her that I couldn't help him out with that problem. Then I said good-bye. Nervous? What does he think I'll do, bite him?

116

I let the pencil drop. It rolled away from me on the mattress. I'd been scribbling so furiously that my wrist was starting to hurt. Not that it was surprising. This particular diary entry was over twice as long as any I'd ever written, and I still hadn't finished. I'd also written it in the same amount of time it normally took me to write about four words.

Sighing, I shoved the diary aside and rolled over, stretching out on my back across the unmade bed.

My gaze accidentally wandered across my bookshelves to my favorite—no, *formerly* favorite—sculpture: the clay hand palming the miniature basketball. The mere sight of it filled me with rage. I was *not* going to make the first move to patch things up with Miles. I was not going to call him and apologize. If he felt bad, fine, he could call me. But it was *his* fault.

I squeezed my eyes closed, desperately struggling to shut reality out of my carefully constructed little world. But it was no use. I was lying to myself again, and I knew it. I couldn't help it, though. At this point, lying to myself and being angry was a lot better than the alternative, which was admitting the truth and sobbing for about the hundredth time in a week.

Well, even if I *was* forced to face the truth, at least I knew that Miles was thinking about me as well. And from what China had told me, he wasn't exactly whooping with joy either. So there was a hope of salvaging at least *some* sort of relationship. Maybe if we made up and started over as friends again, I'd forget about being in love with him. Maybe I'd get so proficient at being his friend that I wouldn't be able to be anything else.

Who am I kidding?

Tears welled up behind my closed eyelids. I blinked a few times. In the blurry, watery fog, I could still see the uncertain shape of the hand and basketball. Everywhere I looked, there was some reminder of Miles: a sculpture he had made for me, photographs of the two of us, a sweatshirt he had lent me . . . there was just no escape. If I wanted to forget about being in love with him, I'd have to move into a different house, maybe even to a different country.

"Sam?"

I jumped. Beth was standing just outside my closed door. I hadn't even heard her out there.

"Sam, can I come in?" she asked.

I sniffed loudly, rubbing my eyes with my palms. "What is it, Beth?"

"I, uh, just wanted to see if you were all right."

"I'm fine," I croaked. "I'm just tired."

"You're *always* tired," she said. "Something's going on."

I had to laugh, in spite of the fact that my eyes and cheeks were still wet. For some reason, Beth had seen fit to appoint herself as my shrink lately. It *was* very sweet, even if it was extremely annoying.

The door suddenly flew open. "*See?*" she said, pointing at me as though she had just made some momentous discovery. "You're crying. What's wrong?"

"I'm not crying, Beth," I stated, sitting up straight. "There's something caught in my eye."

She made a face.

Our eyes met. All at once, we both started cracking up.

It felt pretty nice to lose myself in hysterics, if only for a few seconds. Finally I took a deep breath. I wiped my face with my sleeve, then leaned back against the pillows. "Beth, really, I'm fine," I said, sniffing again. "It's no big deal."

Beth shook her head. "Well, it's gotta be a bigger deal than you're letting on, because you've been acting like a total freak all week."

"Gee, that's nice," I said dryly. "You really have a knack for cheering people up."

"Seriously, Sam." She walked over and sat on the edge of my bed. "What's up?"

"How have I been acting like a total freak?" I asked, avoiding the question.

She shrugged. "Well, you haven't yelled at me once since last Thursday. You've been a total pushover about everything. Even Mom noticed."

I raised my eyebrows. "And that's *bad?*"

"No . . . it's just not like you," she said. "And to be honest, it's a little scary."

"Hmmm." I started to smile. "So you're scared by the fact that I'm *not* yelling at you anymore. Now who's the real freak in this scenario?"

"Sam, come on, be serious. It has something to do with Miles, right?"

I blinked. "What makes you think that?"

119

She threw her hands in the air. "It doesn't take a genius to figure it out, Sam!" she cried. "First of all, you two got into a screaming fight last week. Then you fell into this weird, zombielike coma. I've heard you crying in here a bunch of times. And I'm pretty sure he hasn't called once since then, at least not—"

The phone started ringing. I breathed a secret sigh of relief. It was most likely one of Beth's little teenybopper friends, calling up to giggle for the next couple of hours. Beth would leave me alone, and I would be free to wallow once again in self-pity. I hastily grabbed the phone off the hook. "Hello?"

There was silence at the other end.

"Hel-*lo?*" I demanded impatiently. "Who is it?"

"Sam?" a tentative voice asked.

A wave of nausea gripped my stomach. It was Miles.

"Who is it?" Beth hissed.

I shook my head. My mouth was moving, but I was incapable of forming words.

"Sam?" Miles asked again. "Are you there?"

"Yeah, yeah," I eventually managed. "I'm here."

"Who is it?" Beth persisted.

I cupped my hand over the mouthpiece. "It's Miles!" I whispered fiercely. "Now shut up!"

Beth frowned. "What does he—"

"Miles?" I said quickly, uncovering the mouthpiece. I waved my hand at Beth, as if shooing away an annoying pet. "Get out of here," I hissed.

I heard Miles sigh on the other end. "Hey, Sam, if this is a bad time—"

"No, no, not at all." I glared at Beth. For some reason, she wasn't budging. "I'm just waiting for my darling little sister to leave the room," I growled.

Beth stuck her tongue out at me. But finally she got up and marched out the door, slamming it behind her. I shook my head. One of these days I was going to have to teach her some basic manners—like knowing when to butt out. "Miles?" I said again.

"Yeah, I'm here."

I swallowed. "Uh . . . how's it going?"

"Not bad."

There was a long pause. I waited for him to say something more, but he didn't. The silence continued. I could hear the clock ticking in my room. *Tick-tock, tick-tock . . .* it seemed to drag on and on, interminably. Finally I couldn't take it anymore. "Look, Miles, I—"

I broke off when I realized that he had started talking at the exact same time.

He laughed softly. "You first," he said.

"No, you," I insisted.

"Well, okay." He took a deep breath. "All I want to say is that . . . this sucks. I feel like total crap. I mean, it's stupid that we aren't talking to each other. And I know that a lot of it is my fault." His voice rose as he went along. "What I'm really trying to say is that I'm sorry. You're my . . . you're my best friend, Sam." He stumbled awkwardly over the words. "I want to keep it that way."

121

Much to my surprise, I found that I was weeping by the time he finished. I hadn't even noticed when it started. *So much for coming across like a tough jock chick,* I thought. But for once I didn't care that my defenses were down. I didn't even care if Miles heard me.

"Sam, are you all right?" he asked.

"Yeah." I sniffled. "I'm fine. I'm just really happy you called, I guess."

He laughed softly. "Really? That's, um . . . an interesting way of showing it."

I laughed along with him. "Hey, don't let it get around that I'm a sensitive type, all right?" I said. My laughter grew. It was as if a poisonous cloud had been lifted and I could once again bask in the healthy glow of the hot sun. Miles and I were still best friends, even after everything that had happened. Our friendship could survive anything. And in spite of how I truly felt about him, I knew that our friendship—above all else—was the most important thing in my life.

"So, do we have a truce?" he said. "Can we let bygones be bygones?"

"Definitely," I breathed. "I mean, *I'm* the one who acted like a complete jerk. If you're willing to forgive me, then . . . I don't know. I ought to throw you a ticker-tape parade."

"*Now* you're talking. But Sam, seriously. If there's something you want to talk about, all you have to do is tell me, okay? You don't have to hide anything from me. You can tell me anything you want—whenever." He paused. "All right?"

I swallowed, suddenly nervous. "Uh . . . all right," I said, not quite sure how to react to that. What was he getting at? Did he know I was hiding something from him?

"We don't have to get into this now," he added quickly. "But I want to see you, all right? I want to talk to you in person."

I nodded, very relieved he had let it go at that. "Yeah, I really want to see you too," I said. I hoped I didn't sound *too* eager. I thought for a moment. "Hey, you know what? Tomorrow's our season opener. We're playing Dunbar at three o'clock in the gym. Why don't you come? You can cheer wildly for me, then we can hang out after the game."

"Now *there's* a good idea," he said. "We can catch up on the past week, *and* I can criticize your outside shot, all at the same time."

I laughed. His old, familiar sarcasm was back. It was like hearing a long-forgotten favorite song. "Miles, you know that won't be necessary. My outside shot is so sweet—"

"That it'll give me cavities," he interrupted. "Yeah, yeah. That's about the billionth time I've heard that one, Sam. You really need to work on finding some new lines for this season. I think that one was already old before the NBA was invented."

"Well, we mock what we do not understand, Miles," I said jokingly. "And *you*, my friend, do not understand how to shoot an outside jumper."

"That doesn't stop me from being a good critic, though," he retorted, and I could tell from the sound of his voice that he was smiling. "You'll thank me later. If I didn't tell you about your weaknesses, who would? Besides, these kinds of things are going to be important in the long run, you know, when I'm your agent."

"Oh, right." I grinned into the phone. "I forgot about that."

"Well, it's high time you remember." He sighed. "But listen, Sam?"

"Yeah?"

"Let's never, ever fight again, okay? I don't know if I could survive another eight days without having these meaningless, idiotic conversations."

My eyes immediately started watering again. I gulped and shook my head. It was pathetic. I was worse than a newborn. Miles could have told me the five-day weather forecast and I would have started bawling.

"I'm glad I called," he said after a moment. "You know, it's funny. You and me . . . we don't really do so well when we're apart."

"I know," I whispered. I closed my eyes, trembling slightly. "I know."

"So look, I'll see you tomorrow at three, all right? Good luck. I hope Coach Manigault's torture sessions will pay off."

I drew in my breath, trying to gather what little composure I could to manage a farewell. "I'm sure they will. Good-bye, Miles."

"Good-bye, Sam."

I placed the phone back on the hook. My entire body was quivering and tingly, as if seized by a fast-moving current.

Was it possible? Did he actually feel the same way I did?

Maybe. Not only had we made up, but he had said something so wonderful, so perfect, so extraordinarily beautiful that I had nearly lost control of myself. And I hadn't even known I needed to hear it so badly.

"You and me . . . we don't really do so well when we're apart."

Yes, it really *was* possible. He had said it for the both of us. We were meant to be together. China Henry was clearly a thing of the past. Now that I thought about it, he hadn't mentioned her once during the entire conversation. He must have finally come to his senses. I knew he'd get over her eventually. His obsessions came and went, but one thing remained constant: *us.*

And why not? It made perfect sense. If I needed him, why wouldn't he need me? We had both spent so much time and effort denying that we were a couple that we were blind to the fact that it was true. Everybody else had been right about us all along—everybody except Miles and me. And we couldn't afford to keep living the lie. *That* was why he wanted to see me in person. *That* was why he had told me that I didn't need to hide anything from him anymore.

"Hey, Beth?" I called, too excited to keep quiet.

"Yeah?" came the faint reply.

"Guess what? You don't have to worry about me anymore. As of this moment, I'm going to start yelling at you again."

TWELVE

MILES

I ARRIVED AT the art studio a little past noon on Saturday, feeling better than I had felt in a long, long time. Everything in my life had suddenly fallen into place. I was sculpting well—better than I had ever sculpted in my life, in fact. Fall semester was proving to be a breeze. Most important, Sam and I were best friends again.

And I happened to be dating the most beautiful girl at Jefferson High.

Maybe my good mood also had a little to do with the fact that for once I had the studio all to myself—at least for the time being. Mr. Washington had agreed to keep it open for us on the weekends, now that we were seniors. Apparently, being a senior meant we were responsible enough to be on school property without supervision. Of course, we weren't allowed to use the kiln, or to use any materials that weren't expressly designated for us, or even to set foot outside the studio door for any other reason than to go to the bathroom. But it was something.

I yanked the clay table out into the middle of the floor, then opened the refrigerator door and took a look at my work. For the first time, I smiled. It was almost finished. After having spent the first week of school starting over and over, I had finally managed to create something that I actually liked. Now that China and I were spending so much time together, I was truly able to commit every single detail of her face, from every angle, to memory. My smile broadened. Yes, shaping the clay had become much easier as of last Friday night.

Now I just had to put on the final touches: the little tuft of hair at the end of her braid, her nose ring, and her eyelashes. It would take about three hours—just the right amount of time before Sam's game started downstairs in the gym. Which reminded me that I still needed to call China to invite her. She didn't even know that Sam and I had made up. I'd tried calling her the night before, but for some reason, her phone had been busy for hours. Maybe her parents had left it off the hook or something.

Using both hands, I delicately lifted the bust out of the refrigerator and placed it on the clay table, then headed to the pay phone at the end of the hall.

Kirk was coming up the stairs. I smiled victoriously. "First come, first served, my man," I said. "Don't even *think* about sliding the table back."

He just rolled his eyes, as if he had absolutely no intention of listening to me. "Sure, Miles. Where are you going?"

I pointed to the phone as he passed me. "I'm calling China to see if she wants to watch the girls' basketball team play this afternoon," I said. "You feel like going?"

Kirk froze. "Whoa, whoa. Wait a second. Let me get this straight. You're calling *China* to see if she wants to go watch *Sam* play?"

I shrugged casually, but I was smiling. "Yeah. What's the matter with that?"

"You and Sam are on the skids, and you're trying the moves on this new girl by taking her to your girlfriend's game?" He laughed. "I gotta hand it to you, Miles. Nobody operates quite the way you do."

I shook my head. "You know, Kirk, you never cease to amaze me. First of all, I don't need to put any moves on China. We're already past that stage."

He sneered, just as I knew he would—but he didn't try to say anything.

"Second of all," I continued, "Sam and I were never on the skids, because—and I want to make this absolutely clear for the forty millionth time—we were never going out."

Kirk chuckled. "Whatever, man." He turned and kept walking. "I don't want to get involved in this one. It's gonna get real messy."

"Hey, Kirk," I called after him. "Remember how I told you that you'd be the first to know when

I got a girlfriend? Well, I'm letting you know. I have a girlfriend. And she isn't Sam Scott. You hear that? *She . . . isn't . . . Sam . . . Scott.*"

"Whatever you say, Miles." His voice echoed down the long, empty hall. "But if I were you, I'd be careful. Don't take China to that game, and don't let Sam see that sculpture you're making. That's my advice. But hey, what do I know?" He disappeared into the studio.

Not much, I answered silently. Even after he found out about Friday night, even after he found out that China was the "fictitious girl"—even after he found out that I had *kissed* her—he still thought I was sneaking around behind Sam's back. It was incredible. Maybe believing in that kind of thing made his life more interesting or something. I dropped a quarter into the slot and dialed China's number.

She picked up after just one ring. "Hello?" she asked eagerly.

"Hey, it's me," I said.

There was a pause. "Who?"

I frowned. "Miles. You know, the guy you eat lunch with every day?"

"Oh." She sounded vaguely disappointed. "Hey. What's up?"

"Not much." I paused. "Are you all right?"

"Yeah," she said quickly. "It's just that I was . . . um, kind of expecting someone else."

"Oh." I felt a mild pang of anger. "Who?"

"Look, it's no big deal," she said flatly.

130

"Hey, is something wrong?" I demanded, my good mood now forgotten. "Or are you just being rude to me for no particular reason?"

She sighed. "Listen, Miles, I'm sorry. It's just . . . I have a lot on my mind right now."

"A lot on your mind?" The distant tone in her voice was one I'd never heard before—and it frightened me. "You can tell me about it, if you want."

"You'd probably get mad," she said after a moment.

"I already *am* mad. What's going on, China?"

She didn't say anything at first. I heard her fumbling with the phone at the other end. Finally she took a deep breath. "I spoke to Connor last night," she said.

"What?" I barked. Searing rage flashed through me. "Was *that* why your phone was busy for so long?"

"No, no—it's just that after I spoke to him, I didn't really feel like talking to anyone. I left the phone off the hook."

I licked my lips. My mouth was suddenly dry. "Did you ever think that *I* might feel like talking to *you?* It was Friday night. You could have left a message. I must have called your house a hundred times."

"I'm sorry," she said simply. "What do you want me to say?"

"Well, what did you guys talk about?" I demanded. "You were hoping to hear from Connor just now, weren't you?"

"See?" she mumbled. "I knew you'd get mad."

I laughed harshly. "What do you expect, China? You're telling me that you'd much rather talk to your ex-boyfriend than to me."

"I never said that," she protested.

I shook my head, running my hand through my hair. "Look, if you want to talk to Connor, that's your business. But you don't have to keep it a secret."

"I'm *not,*" she stated.

"So what did you guys talk about?" I repeated.

"It really wasn't that big a deal, Miles," she replied tiredly. "He just wanted to know if I was going to the Equinox Fest today."

"The what fest?" I asked—but I was thinking, *If it wasn't a big deal, then why did you leave the phone off the hook?*

"The Equinox Fest. You've never heard of it?" There was just the faintest hint of disdain in her voice.

"No, China, I haven't," I growled. "Enlighten me."

She sighed again. "It's pretty big. It's this huge outdoor concert they have twice a year on the quad at UT, right off Guadalupe. They call it Equinox Fest because it's held on the equinox. You know, those days of the year—"

"I know what the equinox is, China," I interrupted.

"Well, excuse *me.*" Her voice hardened. "Anyway, all the best local bands play there, and this is the first time Connor's band has been asked to play. So it's kind of a big deal for him. That's all. I was actually planning to invite you, you know."

132

I paused, resisting the temptation to say, *Sure you were*. I began pacing back and forth in front of the phone. I couldn't help but feel hurt and jealous and powerless, and it only infuriated me even more. Finally I took a deep breath. "Well, I'd love to go to the Equinox Fest, but I already have plans," I said in as neutral a tone as I could manage. "I'm going to see Sam play in a basketball game today. As a matter of fact, I was calling to invite you to come with me."

"I thought you guys were in a fight," she said.

"I thought you and Connor had broken up," I snapped.

"We *have* broken up, Miles," she said. "But I did go out with him for almost a year, you know? It's not like I want him to drop off the face of the earth."

Anger swelled up within me again. How hypocritical could she get? All that stuff she'd told me the week before—all that stuff about not really missing Connor, about never thinking about him when she was with me—had it all been a lie? I was afraid to open my mouth. I was afraid I'd start screaming at her.

"So what happened with you and Sam?" she asked.

"Nothing," I muttered. "We just realized that it was stupid to fight. Now things are back to normal. We're best friends again."

"Well, good for you." She didn't sound too thrilled about it. In fact, her tone was distinctly sarcastic. "So, do you *have* to go to this game?"

My forehead creased. "Yeah," I said firmly. "I have to go."

"That's perfectly understandable," she said slowly.

"In the same way that *I* have to go to this concert."

"The same way?" I struggled to keep from shouting. "Give it up, China. Sam is my best friend, not my ex-girlfriend."

"Okay. Fine. Look, what time does this basketball game start?"

I swallowed, calming slightly. "Three o'clock."

"Good," she said. "Connor's band isn't scheduled to go on until five. Now, how long are basketball games? About two hours, right?"

"More or less," I replied grudgingly. "Unless there's overtime."

"Assuming there *isn't* overtime, then the two of us can do both, right?"

"Right." I knew what she was getting at, but for some reason, the compromise didn't make me feel any better.

"So there you have it. *I'll* go to the game with you, and when it's over, *you'll* come to the concert with me. All right?"

I knew I didn't have a choice. Anyway, there was no way I'd let her go to that concert alone. "Fine," I mumbled.

"Good. Now, where should I meet you?"

"At the gym. I'll be sitting up at the top of the bleachers, at around midcourt."

"Sounds good. I'll be there at three." And with that, she hung up.

At 3:20—well into the first quarter—China still hadn't arrived.

I slouched back against the concrete wall at the top of the wooden bleachers, grumbling to myself. Luckily, I was isolated from everyone else by at least five rows. All the other people who had come to see the game—maybe twenty at most, all of them parents and siblings—were bursting with school spirit. By comparison, I felt like the Grinch.

At least I was *there*, though, and that was all that mattered as far as Sam was concerned. Before the tip-off, she had looked up in the stands and given me a big, friendly wave. For that brief moment, my sour mood had lifted. But now that the ball was in play and there was still no sign of China, I was bitter once again.

I made a feeble attempt to concentrate on the game, but it was hopeless. China had probably just skipped coming to the gym altogether and gone straight to the concert. I knew it. I'd known it ever since she hung up. And I had *still* gone back to the art studio and finished working on her bust.

Suddenly the bleachers began to rumble with a rhythmic *stomp, stomp, stomp*. I frowned, looking for the source of the noise, then my eyes widened.

China had actually shown up.

A confusing mix of shame, relief, and anger coursed through me. She was marching up the steps looking totally bored.

"What's up?" she asked, sliding in beside me. "What's the score?"

"Fourteen to ten, us." *As if you care*, I thought. She was fully decked out in rock concert mode: leather pants, a black T-shirt that looked as if it

135

would have been small on a Barbie doll, and purple lipstick. She *never* wore lipstick.

She glanced around restlessly, looking at everything *but* the court. "They really pack 'em in for these games, don't they?" she muttered.

I didn't take my eyes off the court, even though I wasn't paying attention. "You know, you're sounding more and more like Sam with each passing day."

"Ah, yes, the illustrious Sam Scott," she said flatly. "The basketball star. That's who we're here for. Let's cheer her on."

I glanced at her out of the corner of my eye. What was *that* supposed to mean? But she was looking at her nails.

"You know, if you *watched* the game, you might actually enjoy it," I couldn't keep the sarcasm out of my voice.

She yawned. "I don't know the first thing about basketball, Miles," she said, without even bothering to look up at me.

"Well, I can teach you." I gave her a little nudge with my elbow and pointed toward the floor. It was perfect timing. Sam had the ball; she was dribbling around the perimeter, looking for an open teammate. "See that?" I said as China looked up. "Dunbar is in blue. Jefferson is in white. Sam is number twenty-three. She's *drib-bling.*"

China rolled her eyes, but she laughed.

"So you *do* know something about basketball," I said. "See?"

"I know what *dribbling* means, Miles." China stopped laughing.

"Good. Sam is a guard. That means her job is to handle the ball and find the open person. She's going to either pass or shoot."

I paused. Amazingly enough, China was actually looking at the game. I turned my attention back to Sam, catching her just as she drove past her opponent toward the basket for a layup. The moment the ball left her fingers, her hand was hacked by Dunbar's center—some huge, pasty girl who dwarfed her. A whistle blew. The ball teetered on the rim, then fell in.

"Yes!" I cried.

The small crowd in front of us started cheering wildly.

"You see that?" I asked, nudging her. "Now *that* is quality hoops."

But China's face remained expressionless. "Did something good happen?" she asked vacantly.

I scowled. She was obviously trying to antagonize me. There was no point in playing along. I stood up and began clapping as Sam stepped up to the free-throw line for the foul shot. "Way to go, Scott!" I yelled. "Way to draw the foul!"

Sam smiled up at me. Then her eyes shifted to China. Her face instantly shriveled in a look of pure disgust.

I swallowed. My clapping slowed, then died out.

China cleared her throat. "Uh, Miles? Did Sam know I was coming today?"

I didn't answer. I stood there, staring at Sam in a state of shock as she took the basketball. She dribbled once, then threw up a completely out-of-control shot that clanged loudly off the backboard. The pasty

Dunbar center caught the rebound. I sank back in my seat. Something was seriously wrong. Sam *never* bricked free throws like that.

"Miles?" China asked. "Did she?"

I turned to look at her, swallowing again. "Well, no, but . . ."

She shook her head sadly. "She doesn't look too psyched about it."

I didn't know what to say. China was absolutely right. But it didn't make any sense. Why would Sam care about China's being there or not?

"Listen, Miles, I'm going to go," China said, getting up. She didn't sound angry; she just sounded as if it was the only reasonable solution. "I don't want to cause any more problems between you guys. You can meet me at the concert if you want."

I blinked, still totally bewildered. "You're not causing any problems."

"Yes, I *am*, Miles." She laughed once. "Just look at her. She hates me."

"She doesn't hate you. You guys are friends. She told me—"

"It's not about *us*," China stated, silencing me. "It's about *you*. This is something the two of *you* need to work out." She turned and began carefully descending the steep set of stairs.

"What are you talking about?" I shouted after her. A few of the people sitting in front of us glanced nervously over their shoulders, but I didn't care. "Why would she say that you guys are friends if you're not?"

China paused and looked at me, almost pityingly. "Miles, people always say the exact opposite of what they mean. Especially people in Sam's situation."

I watched as she hurried down the rest of the steps and ran out the door. My mind was reeling. Sam's situation? What kind of situation was that? What about *my* situation? There I was, sitting alone, abandoned by my girlfriend, with my best friend furious at me again for no apparent reason. That morning I'd felt like the king of the world. Why had everything fallen apart?

A piercing whistle blew, wrenching my attention back to the court.

Sam had been called for a foul. She was stamping her feet on the floor, her long red ponytail bobbing furiously. She was throwing a tantrum. She never threw tantrums. Coach Manigault was frantically waving her over to the bench.

This is insane, I said to myself.

Once again I leaned back against the concrete wall.

I realized something at that moment.

For once in his life, for whatever mysterious reason, Kirk Evans had been right. I should have never brought China to this game. Things had definitely gotten very, very messy.

THIRTEEN

SAM

I WAS AWARE that Coach Manigault was yelling at me, demanding to know why I had viciously slapped some Dunbar girl in the arm while trying to steal the ball, but I barely heard her. In any case, her words were totally meaningless. Everything was. The foul, this game, the sport of basketball—*everything*. I had been betrayed in the cruelest, most humiliating way possible. Why should anything matter after that?

". . . gonna have to give you a few seconds on the bench to cool off," Coach Manigault was saying sternly. "All right?"

I looked at her. She was glaring at me with her beady blue eyes, her pudgy face creased with frustration. It struck me in a sort of detached way that she looked far too upset over a measly little foul, in a game that wasn't even *real*. I shrugged, then plopped down at the end of the bench.

"What is your problem, Sam?" she bellowed. "Do you think you're Dennis Rodman or something? Where is this attitude coming from?"

The whistle blew. She gave me one last menacing look—but then, thankfully, she had to turn her attention back to the game. *You want to know where this attitude is coming from?* I silently answered. *Turn around and look behind you. There, at the top of the bleachers. That's where it's coming from.*

Strangely enough, I didn't even feel that upset anymore. After the initial outburst, my rage had almost instantly settled into a stagnant numbness. Maybe it was because I subconsciously realized that acting out my aggressions wouldn't serve any purpose. I had skipped the first three of those four phases of grief that they talk about in Intro to Psych—denial, anger, and depression—and gone straight to acceptance.

Yup, there was no denying it. Miles *didn't* love me. He loved China Henry.

There were a few minor details about the situation that I couldn't quite comprehend, though. What had he hoped to accomplish by leading me on the night before? And if he really *did* want us to be friends, why had he brought *her* to the game when I'd specifically told him that we were going to hang out afterward?

None of these little questions were terribly important, however. Maybe I'd get an answer to them someday—and maybe I wouldn't. In the grand scheme of the universe, the unshakable truth remained: I was out of the picture as far as Miles Wilson was concerned. Six years of my life had been flushed down the toilet with one exquisitely thoughtless gesture.

Against my better judgment, I cast a quick glance over my shoulder at the bleachers. Miles was sitting by himself again. For a crazed, blissful moment, I thought maybe I'd hallucinated the whole thing. But no, I knew I hadn't. Little Miss Alternative Music had probably gotten bored and gone home to watch a *Real World* marathon or something. At least Miles felt guilty enough to stay. Guilt wasn't totally worthless.

"Sam!" Coach Manigault grunted at the other end of the bench. She snapped her fingers at me.

I almost felt like laughing. She already wanted me to check back in. It was absurd. I'd nearly forgotten I was even *at* a basketball game.

"Come on, Sam, hop to it!" she ordered. "You're in for Jessica."

I felt as if I were standing outside my body, watching someone else, as I stood and marched over to the scorer's table.

"And let's see you keep your head in the game," the coach growled.

I nodded. I doubted if I could keep my head in the game, but at least I could try to let my internal autopilot take over. The whistle blew and I trotted back onto the court. Ariel stood on the sidelines, ready to inbound the ball. She flashed me a brief look that was obviously meant to say, *What is your problem? Snap out of it!*

I just shrugged again.

Some short little girl began guarding me. She waved her arms in front of me like some giant, annoying insect flapping its wings. I faked left, then dashed to the right, my sneakers squeaking on the wood floor. Now the girl was gone. Ariel launched the ball in my direction.

The ball seemed to come at me in slow motion. I saw the hoop at the far end of the floor. In one fluid maneuver, I snatched the ball out of the air and began sprinting toward the basket, my feet and the ball pounding on the floor. Adrenaline surged through my body. I suddenly felt unstoppable. *This* was my purpose in life—to drive to the basket, again and again and again, a one-woman battering ram. It didn't matter that the big, stupid-looking Dunbar center had planted herself in front of me. I would just have to go through her.

"Sam, what are you doing?" Coach Manigault shouted in horror from the bench.

But her voice was barely audible. I lowered my shoulder and slammed into the shoulder of the Dunbar center, sending her toppling onto her back. A gasp of pain escaped the girl's lips. I heard the whistle blow and I lost my balance, but managed to get the shot off anyway. As I fell to the floor behind the backboard, I saw the ball circle the rim and fall through the net. I raised my hands over my head in an ecstatic moment of lunatic, self-absorbed triumph.

Everybody was staring at me.

"No basket," the referee called, waving his arms. He grabbed the ball. Even *he* looked stunned. "No basket. Offensive foul."

The Dunbar center pushed herself to her feet, then whirled around and glared at me. "What were you trying to do, kill me?" she demanded. She rubbed her shoulder and winced. "That *hurt*."

I ignored her. Instead, I stood and marched over to the referee. Once more I felt as if I were watching someone else. "No basket?" I heard myself shout. "What are you talking about?"

He didn't say anything. He just looked at me, his eyes slowly narrowing.

Before I could say anything more, Ariel rushed over and inserted herself between us, pushing me away from him. "Sam, what's gotten into you?" she hissed. "Will you chill out?"

"That was a basket, dammit!" I yelled over her shoulder at the ref. "That's the dumbest call I've ever heard!"

The next sequence of events passed in a rapid blur. The referee blew his whistle at me and pointed toward the locker room, indicating I had been thrown out of the game. Coach Manigault stormed onto the court and began shouting at me, demanding to know what was going on. Ariel put her arm around me and whisked me to the exit, advising me to sit in the locker room for a few minutes and collect myself before I did anything else that could possibly get me expelled, hospitalized, or maybe imprisoned.

And then—very suddenly, it seemed—I found myself standing outside the locker room door.

I was all alone. The sounds of the game were muffled and far away.

"Sam?"

No, I *wasn't* alone. Miles had followed me. He was standing at the end of the narrow corridor that led back to the gym, looking at me with an expression I didn't think I'd ever seen on his face before: fear. If it hadn't been so awful, it would have been almost comical. He honestly looked as if he was *afraid* of me.

"Sam, what happened out there?" he asked quietly.

I shrugged. "I got thrown out of the game."

He took a tentative step in my direction. "I know. You, uh . . . you didn't think the ref made the right call?"

"No, I didn't, Miles." I grimaced. "But why do you even care?"

He shook his head. "It's just not like you to knock somebody on her butt and then complain about it." His voice was oddly colorless. "I don't think I've ever seen you do anything like that. You didn't even say you were sorry."

For a moment, a tight feeling pulled at my insides. I *had* knocked somebody on her butt. But it had been the wrong person. I should have knocked Miles on his butt—a long time ago. "Yeah, well, my game has changed a lot recently," I muttered. "It's all about being aggressive and looking out for number one. I don't see why you have a problem with that, Miles. You should be proud. I'm trying to be like you."

He took a few more steps toward me. I could see now that he wasn't exactly looking his best. In the fluorescent light, his face appeared tired and pale. His hair was disheveled and partially hanging in his face. He no longer looked scared; he just looked lost and confused.

"Exactly what is that supposed to *mean?*" he asked.

"What do you think it means?" I demanded.

"Sam, I'm sick of playing games. Just—"

"Well, I'm sick of the way you always try to act stupid," I interrupted. "You're not stupid, Miles. I still know you better than that."

His stare hardened. "Maybe you don't know me that well. Maybe I am stupid. I mean, I was under the impression that we made up. Am I wrong?"

I sighed, then put my hand on the locker room door. "This isn't the time or the place, Miles. I was just ejected from the season opener. I'm not in any condition to talk about something as dumb as whether we made up or not."

"Sam, you got *yourself* ejected from the game. On purpose. And I want to know why."

I shook my head, refusing to listen to his words. "Believe whatever you want to believe. It makes no difference to me."

"It has something to with China, doesn't it?"

At the mention of China's name, I threw the locker room door open and slammed it behind me, then locked it. My heart was racing—and that old, familiar wet sting was coming back to my eyes. There was no way I was going to let Miles see me cry. I wouldn't give him the satisfaction.

"Sam?" Miles said. "Look, I'm sorry—"

"Just go away!" I shrieked.

I heard footsteps approaching in the hall. "What's going on?" Ariel's voice demanded. "Is she in there?"

"Yeah, but she locked the door," Miles replied.

The door shook with three loud knocks. "Sam?" Ariel said, sounding nervous.

"Everybody just please go away," I pleaded in a shaky, whispery voice. "I'll be fine."

I pressed my ear to the door. I heard the faint hiss of their whispering, then a pair of footsteps leaving. I held my breath.

"Look, Sam, can I talk to you?" Ariel asked. Her voice had become much gentler.

I sniffed and wiped my eyes. "Aren't you supposed to be playing right now?"

"It's the end of the first quarter. Just open up, all right?"

I exhaled deeply. I couldn't just barricade myself in the locker room; it was foolish, not to mention crazy. I undid the latch, then stepped aside and slouched down on one of the narrow benches in front of a row of lockers.

The door opened.

"Hey," Ariel said softly. She immediately sat beside me, putting her sweaty arm around my shoulder. "What's going on? Why are you so upset?"

"It's nothing," I murmured. "I, ah, guess I just sort of got carried away. Will you tell that Dunbar girl that I'm sorry? Really, I feel bad."

"Definitely," she soothed. "Don't worry about it. She's fine."

I nodded. "Good."

"Listen, Sam, I know Coach Manigault has been working us way too hard. But flagrant fouls aren't gonna do *anybody* any good. I mean, I've been mad at her too. But she just wants to win, and . . ."

My eyes widened in disbelief. I swallowed, not knowing whether to scream or start cracking up. Ariel thought I was upset because of Coach Manigault. It was incredible. Ariel thought that I was freaking out about my basketball coach—the same way Miles had that fateful Thursday night. I didn't even *care* about Coach Manigault. I *liked* Coach Manigault. Was I that hard to figure out? Did people really think I was the kind of person who could get so emotional over something as trivial as *basketball?*

". . . so I'm gonna head back out there, all right?" Ariel patted my shoulder and stood up. "Just change, go home, and mellow out. Don't even *think* about the game. I'll pick you up later, okay? We'll go see a movie or something."

I nodded, still totally shocked. But at least the urge to cry had subsided.

"Hang in there, all right?" she said. The door closed behind her.

I sat there for a while on that hard bench in the dank, smelly locker room, trying to figure out just what I was going to do with myself. *Hang in there?* I wondered. How on earth was I supposed to do that?

That brief little encounter with Ariel had seriously unnerved me. My sister had been right: I *did* have a shell. It was frightening. It was a shell of protective lies, and it had grown so thick that even my closest friends no longer had any idea what I was really thinking or feeling. And sitting there in those grim surroundings, with the rest of my future in so much doubt, I had a kind of epiphany. Why had I even bothered hiding the truth in the first place? It wasn't as if my life could get any worse. The shell wasn't protecting me anymore. In fact, I doubted if it had ever really protected me at all.

No. It hadn't. I stood up, feeling energized and renewed. The old Sam Scott had been ejected from the game, but a new Sam Scott was going to emerge from the locker room. And the new Sam Scott was going to be honest with herself and everyone else.

The shell was going to come off.

FOURTEEN

MILES

TWENTY MINUTES AFTER I left the gym, I found myself walking down Guadalupe Street in the direction of the University of Texas quad. I hadn't left with the intention of walking *anywhere*. At least, that's what I thought. But obviously, some hidden part of my brain was compelling my feet to move toward China. And I knew very well why. China and I needed to finish our discussion. It had been left totally unresolved.

In particular, that one last comment remained stubbornly lodged in my head: *"Miles, people always say the exact opposite of what they mean. Especially people in Sam's situation."*

The only thing I knew for sure about Sam's "situation" was that she disliked China. I knew there was no denying *that* anymore. It was obvious, from the look on her face, from the way she had slammed the locker room door when I'd mentioned China's name, from *everything*. But there was no reason for it. She had befriended China even before I had. True, she had done it largely, if not solely, on my behalf—but she'd always maintained that she wanted us to go out. Of course, she had also made it clear that she never wanted to hear or talk about China either.

If Sam didn't like China, she could have just *told* me right from the start. It would have saved us both a lot of grief. Was she worried I'd get mad at her? Was she worried I would somehow cast her aside in favor of my new girlfriend? It wasn't as if Sam and China needed to be best friends or anything. Sam was *my* best friend. But it was clearly impossible for me to have a best friend and a girlfriend at the same time.

I frowned as I shuffled past the movie theater. No, as of this moment, I had neither a best friend *nor* a girlfriend. It was weird: I had spent most of my time with China talking about Sam—and until the fight, I had spent most of my time with Sam talking about China.

Now that I thought about it, China had seemed less and less enthusiastic about discussing my problems with Sam as the week progressed. In fact, earlier that day China had seemed downright jealous of Sam, with that snide remark about being "here for the basketball star." *I* was the one who should have been jealous; I was on my way to watch her ex-boyfriend sing in front of hundreds of people.

Phineas Bloom's Vintage Clothing was fast approaching on my right. I couldn't help but think of the last time I had walked past it. On that first date with China—our *only* date—she had told me how lucky I was to have a friend like Sam. Of course, *she* could have just been saying the exact opposite of what *she* meant. Maybe she thought the idea of driving around the country in matching American-flag motorcycle helmets was incredibly lame. After all, it wouldn't have been the only lie she'd told me that night. She'd also told me that she didn't miss Connor.

I stopped outside the shop window. The helmets were still sitting right there in all their glittering glory, exactly as I had seen them last. China probably *did* think Sam and I were losers for wanting to buy them. She was way too hip and self-conscious to go in for something like that. Sam, on the other hand, didn't care *what* people thought. She was always willing to try something—no matter how dorky—just for the fun of it.

I was just about to move on when the front door opened a crack. The old fat guy with the beard and long hair poked his head out.

"How's it goin'?" he asked, with a big used-car-salesman smile. "You come back to buy those helmets?"

"Uh . . . not yet. I was just, you know, making sure they're still there."

"Oh, they're still here," he said. "But not for long. People have been expressin' a lotta interest in those beauties. I can't hold on to 'em forever."

I frowned. "I thought I had a three-month deposit on them."

He shrugged. His smile remained stuck to his face, as if it had been painted on. "Don't worry, you'll get your money back. But if somebody makes a better offer before then . . ."

Yeah, right, I thought. I glanced back at the window. I doubted anyone had expressed any interest in them, but I didn't want to take the chance of losing them either. Sam and I *had* to go on that trip. Our dream was much too important to allow any fight, no matter how serious, to get in the way.

"So whaddaya say?" the man prodded. "You're here now. There's no time like the present, right?"

I hesitated for a moment. My fingers brushed the cash in my front jeans pocket. I had seven bucks and some change. I could put the remaining five down on one helmet and get it for Sam right then. I could even give it to her that day. I could show her that no matter what happened, no matter how bad things got between us, nothing could alter our plans for the summer.

"Can I give you five more now and get one, then get the other one later?" I asked.

He looked doubtful. "I don't know if I can hold on to the other one for you. . . ."

"Five bucks is all I've got, all right?"

"Well, all right." He chuckled. "You want the 'his' or the 'hers'?"

"The 'hers.'"

He disappeared back into the shop and snatched one of the helmets out of the display case, then came back to the door. I peered at it closely. Then I looked at the one that was still in the window. They looked identical.

"Uh . . . how can you tell them apart?" I asked.

He shifted it in his hands and held the back of it up for me to see. At the base of the helmet, in tiny, bubbly, psychedelic black letters, were the words Keep on Truckin'. And right under that, in all capitals, was the word HERS.

I started laughing. "Well, I guess that says it, right?"

"Yup. One for your old lady, and one for you."

I rolled my eyes, but I figured there wouldn't be any point in telling the guy that the helmet wasn't for my "old lady." I fished the five-dollar bill out of my pocket and gave it to him. He put the helmet in my hand. It was surprisingly light. It didn't look as if it would do much good in case of an accident. Oh, well. I'd have to be sure to drive carefully.

"You want a bag for that?" he asked.

"Nah. I want to be seen with it."

He laughed. "I don't blame you. You better come back soon for that other one, you hear?"

"I will." I turned and started walking again. My pace was much faster now. I felt a rush of relief, as if I had finally done something to take control of the situation. I would go find China and finish our chat, then I would go present the helmet to Sam. Everything would be resolved. I could already hear the faint sound of music at the end of the street. I broke into a jog and reached the quad in less than a minute.

The first thing I noticed was a huge spray-painted banner: THE FOURTH ANNUAL EQUINOX FEST. SIX BANDS. TEN BUCKS.

I frowned. China had conveniently forgotten to tell me that it wasn't a free concert. For some reason I'd thought it would be. It should have been. They should have been paying *me* to watch Connor Smith play. But the point was moot anyway: I had less than three dollars on me.

I stood on my tiptoes and looked for her. A large area of the wide, flat expanse of grass had been cordoned off with a temporary wire gate, and people were milling around inside. An elevated stage had been set up in the back, near some trees. There didn't seem to be that many people there yet— maybe a hundred or so. Some reggae band was playing, but nobody seemed to be paying much attention. After a few seconds of trying to find China, I gave up and walked over to the entrance, where a guy in his early twenties was sitting at a table collecting money and stamping peoples' hands.

"Hey," I said. "Is it okay if I just go in and look for someone? I'm not gonna stay."

"That's an original one, kid," he said flatly. "Ten bucks. Cool helmet, by the way."

"Uh, thanks. I'm serious, though. I just want to find someone." I put the helmet on the table. "I'll leave this here with you."

He leered at me. "It's not *that* cool. I'm still gonna need ten bucks."

I frowned. I thought about arguing but decided against it. Instead, I wandered off to one side and looked through the gate into the crowd again. If I didn't spot her, I'd just take off. . . .

There she was, standing near the stage, maybe fifty feet away, talking to a guy with platinum blond hair. It was Connor, of course. Who else?

"China!" I shouted, waving the motorcycle helmet above my head. "China!"

It seemed as if everyone *but* China turned their heads—but finally she stopped talking and squinted at me. Connor did too. Even from where I was standing, I could tell that he wasn't overjoyed to see me. China patted his arm, then came walking over. She didn't look too happy either.

"I didn't think you were coming," she said when she reached the gate.

I shrugged. "Yeah, well, Sam got thrown out of the game. There wasn't much point in hanging around to watch the rest of it."

China raised her eyebrows. "What happened?"

"She argued with the ref. Listen, uh, can you come out here and talk? I feel kind of funny talking through this fence."

She fiddled with her braid and looked back over toward Connor. "I don't know," she mumbled. "Connor's band got bumped up to the four o'clock spot. They're gonna go on any minute. Why don't you just come in?"

"Because I don't have ten bucks."

"Well, can't you just go to a bank machine?" she asked distractedly.

"Look, forget it," I said, sighing. "Let's just talk right here. I can pretend like I'm visiting you in prison or something."

"You should really try to come in," she said, unable to keep from looking longingly across the crowd. It was obvious that she had no desire to talk to me. "This is a big deal. Connor told me that some guys from a few independent record labels are gonna be here."

"Neat," I replied with a big, phony smile. "You know what they say. The next big thing is gonna happen right here. Austin is the next Seattle."

She nodded without a trace of humor. "Yeah, that's what everyone says."

I shook my head, suddenly feeling very depressed. "Maybe it'll happen on this very day," I muttered. "Maybe Connor Smith will pave the way."

She didn't respond. Instead, she glanced at the helmet. "I thought you were gonna wait until Christmas to get that," she said.

"I wanted to get it sooner," I said simply.

"And why's that?" There seemed to be a new, penetrating tone in her voice. She was staring at me now.

I frowned. "Because I want to patch things up with Sam."

All at once, for no apparent reason, China smiled. It was that same sad smile she had given me that day at lunch when she had spied Connor across the cafeteria. "Miles," she said slowly, "if you want to patch things up with Sam, why are you here with me?"

"We have some stuff we need to talk about, China," I insisted.

"Well, whatever it is, it's definitely not as important as what you need to talk about with Sam." She paused. "Miles, you're in love with her."

My jaw dropped. Where had *that* come from?

"Right?" she asked.

"Whoa—wait a second." The blood drained from my face. I felt sick to my stomach. "You're not making any sense. That's the craziest thing I ever heard."

"Is it?" she murmured.

"What makes you think I'm in love with Sam?" I gasped.

She took a deep breath. "Because all you ever talk about is her. She's always on your mind. And you're constantly comparing me to her, Miles."

I shook my head, outraged. "I never—"

"It's true, Miles. You know it is. You're always like, 'That sounds like something Sam would say,' or 'You're sounding more and more like Sam.'" China laughed. "It's sweet, but I'm not the one who should be hearing it. Sam should be."

I paused, gripping the helmet tightly—so tightly I thought I might actually crush it. This conversation was unraveling much too fast. Maybe I had made a few comparisons between the two of them, but that kind of thing was natural, right? After all, they were both girls; they were both the same age; they both went to the same school. . . . Besides, China had compared *me* to Connor. She'd told me that I didn't like to hide stuff. I couldn't think of any other specific instances, but I was sure there were some.

"You're a really incredible guy, Miles—I mean it," she continued. "But you shouldn't be wasting your time trying to convince yourself that you're interested in me. It's not fair to either of us."

"But I *am* interested in you!" I cried.

China just laughed again. "That's a nice thing to say. But it's just not true. I think if you really take a good look at yourself, you'll see that I'm right."

My head kept shaking back and forth. She was wrong; she had to be. So I'd gotten a little irritated with her at the basketball game. But I'd been obsessed with her ever since I laid eyes on her in the hall that first day of school. I'd spent every afternoon sculpting her features in intimate detail. If I showed her the bust, she would understand. She would know exactly how I felt.

The band stopped playing. There was scattered applause from the crowd. China looked over her shoulder. "Look, Miles, I should probably be heading back over there. I'll call you later, all right?"

"Wait, wait," I begged. "Listen, stop by the studio after the show is over, all right? There's something I want you to see."

She sighed. "Miles, I—"

"Please," I whispered. My voice was strained. "It's important."

"But I might not be over there until, like, seven o'clock."

"That's okay," I said. "Just be there."

Finally she nodded. "All right, Miles," she agreed, and there was no disguising the reluctance in her voice. "I'll be there."

FIFTEEN

SAM

WHEN ARIEL'S JEEP pulled up in front of my house at around five-thirty, my desire to unleash the honest new Sam Scott upon the world had dwindled considerably. Now I just felt lonely, miserable, anxious, and, above all, embarrassed. I had behaved like a total psycho that afternoon. Not only that, I had actually *hurt* someone. Every time I thought about that poor girl falling to the floor, I shuddered with shame and self-loathing. I doubted if Coach Manigault would even keep me on the team after that—not that I could blame her.

"How's it going?" Ariel asked as I clambered into the passenger side. "You feeling better?"

"Yeah," I lied. Already I felt the shell closing over me again, concealing my true emotions. "Did you tell that girl I was sorry?"

Ariel nodded, then put the car in gear and started down the road. "Yeah. She was fine, Sam.

Really. I think she was more shocked than hurt."
She bit her lip. "We all were."

"I know, I know," I groaned. I stared out the window at the passing houses, tinted gold in the brilliant late afternoon sun. "I don't know what I was thinking."

"We won, by the way," Ariel said after a minute.

Whoops, I thought. My face reddened. I had obviously made a mistake by not asking. "Good," I replied, trying hard to sound enthusiastic. "What was the score?"

"Sixty to fifty-seven. It was a close one, all the way to the end. Jessica isn't nearly as good an outside shooter as you are, but she came through in the clutch."

I nodded, keeping my eyes glued to the passing scenery. "Her shot has improved a lot," I murmured. "And she's good at getting the ball inside. She'll make a good starter."

"And what's that supposed to mean?" Ariel demanded.

I glanced at her briefly, struck by the sudden hardness of her tone. "Uh, nothing," I said.

She frowned. "You aren't thinking about quitting, are you?"

"No, no—not at all," I said. I turned back to the window. "It's just that . . . I mean, do you really think Coach Manigault is gonna want me back after what happened?"

Ariel laughed. "Are you kidding? If anything, you earned her respect. Not that she would ever admit it. But you showed her you aren't soft. That's the key to her new attitude."

"Not soft?" I muttered. "Too bad she's in for a big disappointment."

There was another moment of silence. I felt as if Ariel's eyes were boring into the back of my head. "Sam, what happened out there today?" she asked. "I mean, *really?*"

I swallowed. If there was ever a time to reveal myself, that was it. Ariel had given me the perfect opportunity. But when I opened my mouth, the words were slow in coming. "I guess it was a lot of different things all coming together at once," I finally said. "And none of them really has anything to do with basketball."

"It's not something serious, is it?" she asked, sounding alarmed.

I laughed gravely. "Well, it kinda depends on how you look at it. I'm not dying or anything."

She was silent, waiting for me to go on.

"Hey, uh, Ariel?" I said cautiously.

"Let me guess." She smiled. "You want to ask me a weird question."

"Sort of." I looked at her again. "Do you think of me as somebody who puts up a front?"

Her forehead creased. "What do you mean?"

"Like . . . Let me put it this way. Do you think of me as somebody who tries to come off like a tough jock chick?"

She laughed confusedly. "A 'tough jock chick'? Those aren't the words that leap to mind. Why? Did somebody call you that?"

"My sister, actually," I grumbled.

The Jeep slowed to a stop as we approached a red light, and she turned and looked me in the eye. "*That's* what's bothering you?"

I lifted my shoulders. "That's part of it, I guess. I mean, I don't know—do you ever think that playing basketball makes us unattractive? Like, do you think that guys don't take us seriously because they think we're tomboys?"

She didn't say anything. She was staring at me as if I were completely deranged. Suddenly the car behind us began honking loudly. Neither of us had noticed that the light had turned green.

Ariel put her foot on the pedal, and the Jeep lurched forward. "Sam, do you realize how ridiculous you sound right now?" she asked, hunching over the wheel. "I can personally name about twenty guys who would sell their souls to go out with you."

I shook my head. "It's not *that*. I mean, that was a dumb question. Anyway, *you're* the one everybody lusts after."

"Please," she moaned. "Sam, you are drop-dead gorgeous. Playing basketball doesn't change that. If anything, it helps. It keeps you in perfect shape."

"Well, that's beside the point," I said impatiently. I drummed my fingers on my knees, feeling overwrought and frustrated. I desperately needed to make myself understood to *someone*. "Listen, Ariel, can you keep a secret?"

"Of course I can."

I closed my eyes, took a deep breath, then blurted: "I think I'm in love with Miles."

I looked at her, expecting to see an expression of shock on her face. But she was just concentrating on the road, totally unfazed. In fact, she was smiling.

"I hate to break it to you, sweetheart," she said mildly, "but that's no secret."

"It's not?" I cried.

"Sam, I've known that about you guys for years. Everybody knows."

I shook my head. "But you never said anything. I mean, you've never bothered me about it the way other people do."

She laughed. "That's because I see how much it gets on your nerves."

I sank into my seat, but I couldn't help laughing as well. So the confession wasn't as terrible and earth-shattering as I had anticipated. In fact, it *was* pretty obvious, now that I thought about it. Torturing myself hadn't done a bit of good. But that still didn't do anything to ameliorate the situation.

"Sam, you broadcast it every time you look at him," she said matter-of-factly. "And when I brought up the fact that he's seeing China what's-her-face, you looked like you were going to kill me." She paused, then began nodding. "Now I get it. *That's* what this is all about."

"I just don't understand what he sees in her," I mumbled.

Ariel shrugged. "Believe me, Sam, this little

fling of his isn't gonna last very long. He's probably just trying to make you jealous."

"Well, it's working," I growled. I stared out the window again as Ariel turned onto Guadalupe Street. Suddenly I realized that I had no idea where we were going. "Hey, Ariel, where are you taking me?"

"I'm kidnapping you." She smiled. "I heard about this outdoor concert at UT. I figured we'd go check it out. Does that sound cool?"

I shrugged. "Sure," I said, not really caring *what* we did at this point.

Ariel sighed. "Listen, Sam, I know this sounds crazy and all, but have you ever thought about telling Miles the truth? I mean, as an objective observer, I can see that he obviously feels the same way about you. He's probably scared to do anything about it." She shot me a knowing, conspiratorial look. "Guys are total wimps when it comes to stuff like that."

I scowled. "If he feels the same way about me, then why is he going out with China Henry?"

"He's going out with China Henry to make you mad—so that you'll make the first move," she said confidently, as if she were explaining an irrefutable law of physics. "It's his way of drawing a response out of you. He's worried you aren't gonna do anything about the way you feel, and he's too scared to do anything himself. Believe me, I've seen this kind of thing before."

I was just about to ask her where she had acquired all of this remarkable wisdom, being as she'd never had a relationship with a guy that lasted more than a month, but right at that moment something caught my eye. I gasped, twisting around in my seat. We were speeding past Phineas Bloom's Vintage Clothing. And it looked terribly, terribly wrong.

There was only one red–white–and–blue helmet in the window.

"What is it, Sam?" Ariel asked. "Are you all right?"

"Th–That store back there," I stammered. "It, uh . . ." I couldn't finish.

"Do you want me to stop?" she asked worriedly.

I sank back into the seat, too distraught to answer. Ariel pulled into a University of Texas parking lot and jerked to a halt, but kept the engine running. She looked at me closely. "What is it? You want to go back there?"

I shook my head slowly. I couldn't believe it. The fat old hippie guy really *had* gone ahead and sold one of the helmets. I felt as if a terrible crime had been committed. Miles and I were supposed to have them. We *had* to have them. Giving each other the helmets was going to be our first step to following through with the road trip, of promising ourselves to live out Miles's "big dream." But now we couldn't make that promise. Now everything was different. I was filled with a dreadful certainty that the road trip was never going to happen, that Miles and I would never be friends again, that if only I had agreed to buy those helmets on that Sunday, everything would have turned out differently. . . .

"What is it, Sam?" Ariel repeated.

I looked at her, feeling very empty inside. "I think it's too late," I finally managed.

"Too late for what?"

I swallowed. "Too late for everything."

She leaned back, then licked her lips nervously. "You know . . . I think I'm gonna take you home."

A single teardrop fell from my eye. "I think that's a good idea," I whispered.

SIXTEEN

MILES

I FELT VERY odd, sitting there in the art studio all alone on a Saturday night. When I had returned to school a couple of hours earlier, it had been like walking onto the set of the *Twilight Zone.* The only sound in the vast, empty building had been the loud buzzing of fluorescent lights. I hadn't seen one other person. It was eerie. I was almost tempted to put on one of Mr. Washington's tapes, just to make myself feel more normal and at home.

But I didn't. I continued sitting in stony silence on Mr. Washington's stool. China's bust sat in front of me on the clay table. Sam's motorcycle helmet sat next to it. I had remained virtually motionless all this time, staring at the two objects, trying to figure out how I was going to manage to solve both of the problems in my life. And neither outlook seemed overly promising.

I was proud of the sculpture, at least. Even if I

was a failure in the relationship department, I had succeeded at *this*. That was worth something. There was no denying I had captured the essence of China: the curves of her face, her wide eyes, her innocent smile. The clay had dried quite a bit, and it was beginning to get that chalky, pale, finished look. I had thought about painting and glazing it, but in the end I decided not to. The piece was done. It looked very natural the way it was: just gray, with no adornment. The natural look suited China. Now if only she would show up to see it . . .

At a little past seven, I finally heard the hollow echo of approaching footsteps.

I hopped off the stool and opened the studio door. My hands were shaking. China was plodding down the hall: *click, click, click.* Her head was bent. She looked extraordinarily sad, as if she were on her way to a funeral. *Great,* I thought. I drew in my breath.

"Hey," I called, trying my best to sound cheerful. "Thanks for coming."

"No problem." She didn't lift her head until she reached the door. Then she looked at me without smiling. "How's it going?"

"Okay." I rubbed my palms on my jeans. "How was the concert?"

"It was really, really good. You should have stayed."

I shrugged. A long silence fell between us.

"So . . . what is it you wanted to show me?" she asked.

"Oh." I stepped aside and gestured toward the

clay table without saying another word.

China's lips parted slightly, and her eyes widened. She moved slowly toward the sculpture, looking at it first from one angle, then another, then another. My heart started pounding so loudly I thought she might hear it.

"Wow," she murmured. She glanced up at me. "Can I touch it?"

"Um, not yet. It still isn't completely dry."

She stood over it for what seemed like a very long time. Then she shook her head. "I—I don't know what to say, Miles," she whispered. "It's beautiful. Thank you."

"It's yours," I said, swallowing.

She just nodded.

I bit my lip. "You know, China—"

"Miles, wait," she interrupted gently. "What you've done . . . it's amazing. I can't tell you how amazing." She paused. "But I know it doesn't change the way you feel about Sam."

"But don't you understand?" I asked. My voice was hoarse. "Don't you understand that I never would have made it if I didn't care about *you?*"

She looked at me with a wistful smile. "I *know* you care about me—or at least the person you want me to be. But I'm not sure how real that person is."

"How can you say that?" I cried.

"Miles, you hardly even know me. Think about it. I mean, we've known each other what—two weeks? That's not very long to really get to know someone, is it?"

I stood there staring at her, unable to respond. Two weeks *wasn't* a very long time. But still, I'd felt drawn to China from the first time I'd seen her.

"Let me ask you something," she said. "And I promise I won't get offended. What do you like about me?"

My mind whirled. What *didn't* I like about her? I could think of only one thing: She had once referred to Sam as "that girl." But that was minor—essentially meaningless. Besides that . . . well, she really *did* believe Austin was the next Seattle. That was kind of painful, actually. And she was a little too fashion-conscious, now that I thought about it. She didn't know squat about basketball. Her ex-boyfriend was the biggest jerk on the planet. But other than that . . .

"See what I mean?" she said, smiling. "You can't think of *one* thing."

"I like that you're the most beautiful girl I've ever seen," I blurted stupidly.

She sighed. "You probably don't even know how good that makes me feel. But still, it's not enough." She pointed toward the sculpture. "I mean, there it is, right there. That sculpture sums it up. You love *that*—a girl you invented, with my face. You idealized everything about me because of my looks."

"*What?*" I felt as though I'd been punched in the stomach. I shook my head furiously, refusing to believe her. I couldn't be *that* shallow. "No way. I mean, that day you came in here . . . I knew you were this incredible person. Like the way you

171

freaked out about all of Mr. Washington's tapes. That was so pure and funny——"

"Miles, listen to yourself!" she exclaimed. "That's a perfect example of what I'm talking about. You imagined all of these things about me. Okay, yes, I happen to like funk and soul music. But that doesn't mean anything. If anything, that goes to show that we *shouldn't* be together." She started laughing. "I mean, you call that kind of music 'disco.'"

I started laughing too—mostly out of hopelessness. "Well, okay, we don't have the same taste in music."

"I don't even *know* what kind of music you like!" China cried. "And that's not your fault; it's just that you don't talk about it. But *I* talk about music all the time. It's something I think about a lot. That's probably why I went out with a musician for so long. You see what I'm getting at?"

I blinked. She kind of had a point. *I* didn't even know what kind of music I liked. If something came on the radio that sounded good, I listened to it. Sam was the exact same way. In fact, most of the albums we owned were film sound track compilations. It was sort of pathetic.

Finally I took a deep breath. "So you really don't want to give it a chance?" I asked.

She walked over to me and took my hands. "Miles, I want the chance to be your *friend*. I should have made that clear the day I interviewed you for the article. But Connor had just broken up with me and I was really upset, and I guess I didn't really know what I wanted. I was flattered by your attention. But I honestly don't think we were meant to be a couple."

I looked deep into her gray eyes. I was expecting to feel angry, or upset, or depressed. But I didn't. The truth was, I didn't know *how* I felt. I only knew that it wasn't nearly as bad as I'd thought it was going to be. She was right. We weren't meant to be together. We weren't meant to be anything more than friends.

"Do you still want the sculpture?" I asked quietly.

She squeezed my fingers. "Of *course* I do." She stood on her tiptoes and kissed me on the cheek, then let my hands go. Then she glanced at the sculpture one more time. "Miles, can I ask you something?"

I nodded.

"You never did one of those for Sam, right?"

I shook my head.

She smiled. "Why not?"

"I guess it just never occurred to me," I said.

"But you told me that you *have* given her lots of your pieces—ones that you made especially for her, right?"

My nose wrinkled. "What are you trying to say?"

"What I'm trying to say is that it never occurred to you to sculpt Sam's face for a reason. That's because you always have the real Sam right there in front of you. You never felt the need to create an idealized version of her in your art, because the real thing is as good as it's gonna get."

"Wow," I breathed. "That's pretty heavy." I almost laughed again. "I don't think—"

"Miles, you *adore* that girl. And she adores you. That's one of the sweetest things about you. It's one of the things I always admired about you two from afar."

"I'm surprised you even noticed us," I mumbled.

She threw her hands in the air. "That's *exactly* what *she* said!" she cried. "Word for word! And that's what I'm talking about. Don't you see, Miles? It's amazing. You two are on the same wavelength in a way that nobody I know even comes close to."

I shook my head, feeling very uncertain. "I don't know if that's true. At least, not these days."

China marched over to the clay table, snatched up the motorcycle helmet, and shoved it at me. "Well, *do* something about it!" she yelled.

I carefully took the helmet from her. For what seemed like a very long time, I slowly turned it over in my hands. In a matter of minutes, I'd gone from thinking that China Henry was the love of my life to knowing that she was just a nice girl whom I happened to find incredibly attractive. Of course, that revelation hadn't *really* come in a matter of minutes; it had just taken me that long to realize that I'd been fooling myself all along. And China had been right about something else too: I *had* compared her to Sam. Only now was I starting to see the real reason. Sam was the one who truly possessed all of the qualities I had idealized in China: humor, adventurousness, innocence . . . and beauty.

I *did* adore her.

"You know," I said, "you're right. I *should* do something about it."

China put her arm across my back and steered

me toward the door. "Now you're starting to make some sense, Miles Wilson."

I paused. "I don't know if she'll listen."

"Miles, believe me, she'll listen. I saw her face today at the basketball game. Everything was right there, plain to see. She loves you, Miles. She'll listen."

I wanted to thank her. But I didn't. Because the next thing I knew, I was running down the hall—as fast as my feet would carry me.

SEVENTEEN
SAM

I AM NEVER, ever going to cry again, I swore to myself. *Well, at least not in front of another person.*

I was sitting on my bed. I had locked myself in my room after Ariel dropped me off. I refused to talk to Beth or my mom or anyone else. I should have known that telling the truth wasn't going to do me any good. Of course, at this point, it was too late. Ariel knew about my feelings for Miles, and, according to her, so did everyone else at Jefferson. It was obvious that the humiliation I'd experienced that day was just the start. How could I possibly go to school on Monday after what had happened on the court—*and* in Ariel's car, for that matter?

Not that Ariel would tell anyone that I'd basically had a nervous breakdown, but still, *she* knew. I stood and began pacing around the floor. Maybe I could just flee the country and get plastic surgery and form a new identity. That would be pretty cool, actually. I could be somebody totally different: a Spanish mata-dor, a safari guide in the Amazon . . . anyone but Sam Scott. I couldn't bear to be Sam Scott anymore.

I frowned. Had somebody just rung the doorbell? I thought I'd heard it. I really, really hoped it wasn't Ariel, coming back to offer more condolences. I stepped over to the door and put my ear to it. *Someone* was there, because I heard my mom and Beth muttering quietly, most likely warning the visitor about the precarious state of my sanity. Then I heard heavy footsteps on the stairs. For a horrible instant I thought it might be Coach Manigault, coming to my house to lecture me about sportsmanlike conduct. *That* would be a perfect way to end a perfect day. My mom had no idea I had been ejected from the game.

I stepped back just as there was a loud knock. "Sam?"

I nearly fainted. It was *Miles*.

"Sam?" he asked again.

I clenched my teeth. "Go away. I don't want to talk to you."

"Please, Sam," he begged. "I have something I want to give you."

"I don't *want* anything from you."

"It's an early Christmas present," he said.

I shook my head. If he was trying to be cute, he wasn't doing a very good job. "You're gonna have to do better than that," I spat. "I thought you said you were sick of playing games."

"This isn't a game," he replied. "Please . . . just open the door."

Sighing, I reached forward and undid the lock, then turned my back on him before I even caught a glimpse of his face. "Just put it on the bed, whatever it is," I commanded, folding my arms across my chest.

Miles stepped in front of me and placed something at the foot of the mattress. I refused to look at anything but my feet.

"Don't you even want to see what it is?" he prodded.

"Not really," I muttered.

He grabbed it off the bed and in a single, swift motion jammed it over my head.

"What are you doing?" I shrieked—and then I gasped. Whatever it was, it was padded and fit tightly. On my *head.* But it couldn't be. . .

I tore it off, my heart pounding. I blinked. It *was.* There, in my own two hands, was one of the American-flag motorcycle helmets.

"Merry Christmas," he said quietly.

I looked up at him. He was slouching timidly, with his hands in his jeans pockets, his beautiful brown hair still as disarrayed as it had been in the hall outside the locker room. A doleful smile played on his lips. His brown eyes were drooping slightly, but lurking deep within them was that perpetual, inextinguishable spark.

"How . . . ?" I croaked.

His shoulders lifted a little. "I just figured it was time to buy it."

I gulped, feeling dizzy. "What—What does that mean?" I stammered.

His smile widened just a little. "Um, I guess it means I want you to be protected if the sidecar ever comes loose and you go flying off a cliff."

I shook my head. "Why did you do it?" I breathed.

"Just say that you accept the Christmas present. I have a funny feeling that guy won't accept an exchange or offer a refund."

I laughed in spite of myself and then, of course, I started blinking rapidly. So much for keeping my own promises. I rubbed my eyes with one hand. They were wet, although I supposed I should have been used to the sensation by now. I seemed to be spending most of my waking hours in tears these days. Maybe I was making up for lost time as a child or something.

"Don't worry—I got you the 'hers,'" he said. He pointed to the little logo at the base of the helmet. "You can still get me the 'his.'"

I swallowed, frightened of what I was about to tell him. "But—But somebody else already got it," I said. I sniffed and looked up at him. "There was only one helmet in the window this afternoon."

He cocked his eyebrow, then laughed. "I know. You're holding the other one."

My eyes widened. "*You* were the one who bought it?"

"Of course. Who else?"

I just gazed at him. "It was *you*," I said in amazement.

He took a step forward. "Sam, listen," he said, very seriously. "There's something I have to tell you. I made a very important discovery today."

I nodded. I could hardly breathe.

"I've been very confused these past few weeks," he said. He put his hands on my shoulders and looked me in the eye. "I got everything mixed up. I was dating the person I should have been friends with, and trying to be friends with the person I should have been dating."

The helmet slipped from my hands. It fell onto the rug, but I hardly noticed. "What do you mean?" I whispered.

"I *mean* that I'm in love with you, Sam. And I always have been. I just didn't know it."

I felt as if the entire weight of the universe had just slipped away. The words were so sweet, sweeter than I could have ever possibly imagined. I closed my eyes and threw my arms around him, pulling him toward me and embracing him as tightly as I could. I'd never thought I would hear him say it. I'd never even thought I would survive that night. I buried my face in the soft, warm flesh of his neck. He ran his hands through my hair. I could feel his heart beating right next to mine. And I kept repeating to myself over and over: *Ariel was right. Ariel was right. Ariel was right. . . .*

Finally we stepped apart. He took my hands. I took a deep breath. "I'm glad you told me," I murmured. "Because I was going to have to tell *you*."

"I think you already did," he said. "I just wasn't listening."

I nodded, then paused. "What happened with China?" I asked tentatively.

He shrugged. "We're friends," he replied.

"And now I realize that's all we ever were."

I looked him in the eye. "I love you, Miles."

He pulled me to him again, and our lips melted together in soft kisses. We had never kissed before. I waited for one of us to crack up. Or make a joke. Then, with a shock, I realized just how right it felt—like I'd been kissing him forever. I drew him closer, running my fingers through his hair.

"All right, Sam."

We jumped apart. Miles's face turned beet red. I knew mine must have been even redder. My sister was standing in the open doorway, frowning at us and shaking her head. "Now, are you still gonna try to pretend that Miles *isn't* your boyfriend?"

"I'm not her boyfriend," Miles said quickly. "I'm more than that. I'm her best friend."

She rolled her eyes. "Whatever. Just keep the door shut when you're making out. It makes me want to blow chunks." She closed the door and stomped away.

We looked at each other.

He cracked a smile. I started giggling. The next thing we knew, we were both laughing.

"Isn't that so sweet?" Miles said, clasping his hands together. "It makes young Beth want to blow chunks. I'm sure it will have the same effect on Kirk and Ryan."

"No doubt." I leaned forward and brushed his bangs out of his eyes, as I had done a hundred times in the past. "Hey, Miles, you think Phineas Bloom's Vintage Clothing is still open?"

He grinned. "Yeah. Why?"

"Because I want to get you an early Christmas present. You know, just so we can be sure that we're gonna live out our big dream."

He leaned forward and kissed me lightly on the lips, sending a shiver all the way through my body.

"I think we already have lived out our big dream," he whispered. "Don't you?"

Do you ever wonder about falling in love? About members of the opposite sex? Do you need a little friendly advice but have no one to turn to? Well, that's where we come in . . . Jenny and Jake. Send us those questions you're dying to ask, and we'll give you the straight scoop on life and love in the nineties.

DEAR JAKE

Q: *I have a big problem at my school. There's a guy, Mike, who has had a crush on me since the beginning of the year. We went out for a couple of weeks, but I broke up with him when I realized he was a total creep. Now he wants me back and he keeps getting my friends to ask me out for him. Whenever they tell him no, he threatens to commit suicide! I know suicide is a serious matter and we're only in middle school. Is he serious? How do I handle this?*

FL, Oakland, CA

A: There's one responsible way to take care of this whole situation. Go to an adult you trust and tell him/her about the suicide threat. It could be a teacher, parent, guidance counselor, nurse, principal; anyone with whom you feel comfortable. Mike will probably get called into the guidance counselor's office and he/she will talk to him about his problem. The counselor won't tell Mike it was you who reported the incident if you ask him/her to keep your name confidential.

If Mike is serious about suicide, he'll get the help he needs. If he was just trying to guilt you into going out with him again, he'll be sufficiently scared. He'll know that there are authority figures keeping an eye on him and he'll probably leave you alone.

Q: *I was totally devastated by a guy two years ago. Now, I'm dating this guy named Miguel and he's really great. My feelings for him are even stronger than those I had for the first guy. The thing is, I'm really afraid of being hurt again. Should I stay with Miguel or should I dump him before he dumps me?*
RS, Dallas, TX

A: If you run out and dump Miguel because you were burned by a guy two years ago, you will be making a huge, immense, catastrophic mistake. Although most girls don't believe me when I say this, I'm going to go out on a limb and say it anyway: Guys are not all the same! Just because one immature, idiotic, loser boy broke up with you for the lamest of lame reasons doesn't mean Miguel will do the same. Whenever you enter into a relationship there's a risk you'll get hurt. But don't shut yourself off because of what guy number one did to you. Trust Miguel unless he does something to make you feel that he doesn't deserve that trust. You'll be one step closer to a healthy relationship.

DEAR JENNY

Q: *The strangest thing happened to me the other day. This guy Brett, who I've liked forever, finally asked me out. Then when we went out on the date, he brought his twin brother along. I didn't know what to say. Does dating him mean I have to date his twin? How do I bring up the subject without sounding like I don't like his brother?*

BH, Lake Havasu City, AZ

A: I have never heard of such a thing before. I would wait until your second date. If his brother doesn't come with him, assume he just wanted someone there to make it a group thing. Maybe he felt more comfortable with his brother around. Still, let him know it made you uncomfortable. Just say, "Brett, can I ask you a question?" and then let it out. Chances are he'll have a good, or at least interesting, explanation.

If he does bring his brother on the second date, take Brett aside. Tell him you thought you were dating him, not his brother. Then, unless he gives you a great sob story about how his brother just had his heart broken and has a hard time being alone, and he promises never to do it again, cut your losses. It's hard enough maintaining a relationship with one guy, let alone two.

Q: *My boyfriend, Lou, and I have been together for about six months. We've always been happy but recently he's*

changed a lot. His whole style has morphed. He listens to dif-
ferent music and hangs out with a new crowd. Even his out-
look on life has begun to shift. He's negative about everything.
I don't know if I can love the new him. What should I do?

CG, Jacksonville, FL

A: Talk to him. Hopefully he can still talk to you in the same way he always has. Tell him you're worried about him—that he seems to be taking things very seriously and you don't want him to shut you out. If he's changed friends and his whole outlook, something may be really wrong. Maybe you can help him find a way to work things out.

But if he starts to close you off and treat you in a negative way, you should think about moving on. People always say that if you love someone, you'll love them even if they change. But if he has cut off your mutual friends, started treating you differently, and brings you down when you're around him, there's not much left to love.

Do you have questions about love? Write to:

Jenny Burgess or Jake Korman
c/o Daniel Weiss Associates
33 West 17th Street
New York, NY 10011